Murder With a Hint of PUMPKIN SPICE

LAURA M. DRAKE

WHISPER HOLLOW MYSTERIES
BOOK 1

Note to Readers

The spelling of Bettye's name is intentional. She is named after my grandmother Bettye. I'm letting you know now so you don't assume it's a weird typo in the book.

Acknowledgements

Thank you to my family and friends who support me in this crazy dream of mine, my writing group who helps polish my rough drafts, and the readers who make this job worth doing.

~

This book is dedicated to Michelle, who inspired me to write my own fall-themed story after reading hers. She gave me the push I needed to, for the first time, write a book that wasn't inspired by a dream.

Contents

Chapter 1

Whisper Hollow

"If murder wasn't generally a bad idea, Tate would be dead by now." I rearranged the display table near the front of the bookshop to better display my October reads, books like *Dracula*, *Frankenstein*, and a few Stephen King novels.

Kyle, my part-timer, glanced at me with brows raised, as if he thought I was capable of murder. He shook his head and kept ringing up a teenage girl at the register. Were teenagers that gullible, or did he think all single twenty-eight-year-old women wanted to murder their exes?

"Don't be so dramatic, Harp." My sister's voice rang through my single AirPod. "His posts are annoying; I'll give you that, but you wouldn't kill him. Besides, your breakup was eight months ago," Grace continued. "You said you're over it. You are over him, right?"

"Right." I pushed away the thoughts of my ex. Grace was right. Tate was so eight months ago, and while his cheating sucked, I was better off without him *and* my backstabbing roommate.

"But I wasn't talking about me. I was talking about you." I tucked my short brown hair behind my ear and lowered my voice so I wouldn't disturb the few precious customers wandering around my bookshop. "As my big sister, it's your sworn duty to take out my evil exes."

I could practically hear her rolling her eyes. "You've been reading way too much *Lord of the Rings* again."

At the mention of *Lord of the Rings,* I glanced down at my bare ring finger. Tate had proposed with a replica of the One Ring since we had a tradition of rereading *The Hobbit,* my favorite book, and rewatching the extended version of the trilogy together once or twice a year. At least we'd *had* that tradition before I dumped him for cheating on me.

"First of all, I'm totally offended. There's no such thing as too much Tolkien," I said. "And second of all, that was a Scott Pilgrim reference. Seriously, you're embarrassing me."

"Yes," she said in a deadpan voice. "*I'm* the one embarrassing *you.*"

Her teasing sent a pang of homesickness through me, but I didn't have time for that. Not when I was trying to revive Nana's bookshop. I couldn't let Whispering Pages go without a fight, not after spending hours curled up in my favorite armchair with a book, or the hundreds of memories I had with Nana here.

But then again, what chance did I have? I wasn't a business person. After failing to visit Nana when she needed me and failing in my last relationship, why did I think I could succeed with this?

"Anyway, how's the shop?" Grace said after I let the pause go too long, her voice overly cheerful. She could probably tell I already missed her, and I'd only left a week ago.

"It's great. I've made a lot of progress." I surveyed the room, trying to see the cluttered shop through Grace's eyes. In homage to Nana, I'd gone a little overboard with Halloween decorations. A cauldron of candy rested in the display window next to a life-size skeleton that loomed over a stack of books—one hand in the cauldron as if ready to pass out the candy to customers. Fake cobwebs dangled from the corners and nooks where I'd arranged cozy reading chairs, and pumpkins of various shapes and sizes adorned shelves and tables. I'd even pulled out Nana's gramophone, which I'd spent hours listening to as a kid. It filled the store with a soft, haunting melody.

"Have you met anyone nice yet?" Grace asked.

"Sure," I said. "Nancy has been friendly." And thanks to the wall I shared with her bakery, Sugarplum Delights, my place often smelled like pumpkin spice lattes and apple cider. With a neighbor like that, I couldn't wait to meet the shop owners on my other side.

"Nosy Nancy?"

I snorted at the nickname Grace had given her when we were kids. "Yes, *that* Nancy."

"Anyone else?"

"I haven't met any men, if that's what you're asking."

"I didn't say anything," she said with a laugh that was partially covered by the sound of her kids squealing in the background.

"Yeah, but you were thinking it."

"For the record, I was wondering if you'd made any *friends* out there," Grace said. "But I wouldn't be against you meeting a man."

I frowned at a copy of *The Legend of Sleepy Hollow*—one of Tate's favorite books—then cleared my throat and put it on the table a little too aggressively. "The only guys you can trust are fictional ones."

"Please don't say such depressingly nerdy lines, Harp." Grace sighed and thankfully refrained from giving me her usual lecture about how I needed to learn to trust guys again because *They aren't all scumbags like Tate.* "What about Nana's house?" Grace asked. "Do you feel settled in yet? Is it freaky living in the woods on your own? It always felt like Nana was the sole determining factor between her house being a cute cottage in the woods or a scary cabin in the forest.

Without her there . . . it leans too much into horror movie vibes for my taste."

A laugh slipped out before my sadness muffled it. "No, it isn't scary, but it's weird being there because everything reminds me of her."

"I get it," she said quietly. "It would be hard to be there without her."

"I don't get why she didn't tell us she was sick. We could have visited or—" My throat closed, cutting off the rest of my words.

"I know." Grace sighed. "Nana always did things her way. She probably didn't want us to worry about her, but it doesn't make it easier."

The bell over the door dinged. I stood and turned around to greet the customer. "Welcome to Whispering Pages, where every book has a story to tel—oh, it's you."

"Who is it?" Grace whispered as if the new arrival could hear her through my AirPod.

The man strode into the store, his usual briefcase in hand. This time, he wore a black suit with ostentatious gold cuff links and a flashy tie clip. "I thought we might talk about the bookshop." He ran his free hand over his slicked-back gray hair and gave me a wide smile, like a shark closing in on its prey.

"Who is it, Harp?" Grace repeated.

"It's Mr. James." I kept my voice low. "I gotta go."

"The jerk who keeps threatening to shut down Whispering Pages? Give him the phone. I've got a few choice words for—"

I disconnected the call and caught Kyle's eye before turning my attention to Mr. James, trying to be civil. "What are you doing here again?"

The keyword was *trying*. Very few people got under my skin as easily as Mr. James did. We'd only met twice, and I already loathed the guy.

"I thought we might discuss your grandmother's business."

"How many times do I have to tell you that I'll get you the rent for next month?" *Somehow.*

"I'm a man who judges results, not words." He looked around the shop, eyeing the three customers in the store, then shook his head.

I straightened my shoulders. "And I don't like people telling me what I can and can't do."

"You don't seem to have your late grandmother's business acumen."

"I'll manage." I crossed my arms, trying not to pay attention to how his words echoed my insecurities. A week was far too soon for either of us to know that, but I couldn't stand the thought of failing her shop now. Nana's business was fine when I was a kid, but after looking over the last few years of financial statements, I could see how tight things had been. Maybe it was because Mr. James kept raising the rent, or maybe she hadn't been able to keep up with things due to her illness. Either way, the shop needed help, and my meager savings wouldn't cover it.

He rubbed the bridge of his nose. "It would be in your best interest to vacate the building."

"You mean *your* best interest?" I folded my arms across my chest.

"I'll admit, I have some other ideas in mind for this place. It's a prime location, and there are more fruitful ways I could use the real estate," he added with another pointed look at the near-empty shop. "If you end the lease early, I'll waive the fee."

I ground my teeth. "I don't want to end the lease, and according to the contract, you can't kick me out if I pay on time."

If he ended the lease, there was a penalty for him, which was probably why he was trying to get me to do it.

"And last I checked," I added, "Nana already paid for this month. So, if you don't mind, I should get back to work."

He tipped his hat to me and laid a business card in the skeleton's hand. "Think about it. We could do this quietly and save you some embarrassment, or you can struggle all month and still lose. It's up to you."

Nana's black cat slunk out from under the table and wove between my legs.

Mr. James looked at her, sniffed, and walked out the door.

Jiji meowed for attention, and I bent to pet her. I'd visited the summer Nana had adopted her, and I didn't have the heart to get rid of her. Having her around was almost like having a small piece of Nana around too. Plus, it was nice having company. It kept the cottage from feeling so empty.

After Kyle left for the day, I ran through the closing routine Nana had drilled into me during my summers working in the shop: check the inventory, close the register, clean the shop, and lock up. The nightly deposit made me sigh. While I was grateful for every dollar, I needed to do better if I wanted to keep the bookstore out of Mr. James's greedy hands.

Trying to brainstorm ideas, I stepped outside. Jiji slipped out with me, then disappeared down the alley. She had a habit of doing that. I shook my head and locked the door. The street lamps—dressed in tiny wreaths of dried leaves and miniature pumpkins—stood like sentinels on either side of the street. They flickered on, and their soft glow illuminated the area as the sun dipped closer to the horizon. A chill wind cut through the street, rustling the dead leaves on the ground.

I shivered and wrapped my peacoat tighter around myself, then hurried into Nancy's bakery like I'd done most nights since moving in. I hadn't quite gotten around to picking up more groceries beyond the basics for breakfast.

The wind rustled the lace curtains framing the large windows at the front before I closed the door behind me. I inhaled the scents of spiced lattes, pumpkin pies, and hearty soups, and my stomach gurgled. The soft hum of chatter from the groups of people at the tables filled the air with a pleasant buzz, and the pendant lights cast a warm ambiance on the exposed wooden beams overhead and the vintage baking posters on the walls. Walking into the bakery was like being hugged by a cinnamon roll. It made me feel warm and cozy and at home.

I got in line behind a young couple debating between a flaky croissant and a buttery Danish. The man, whose blond hair and broad shoulders reminded me too much of Tate, laughed at something the woman said and wrapped an arm around her waist.

My heart throbbed at the sight, and I glanced away. To give my hands something to do, I straightened the scarecrow leaning against the small blackboard that announced the daily special.

An elderly gentleman sat at a table near the wall covered by shelves that were filled with jars of homemade jams, preserves, and pickled vegetables. He stared at the vase of sunflowers and dried wheat stalks that stood as his table's centerpiece. His deep-set eyes crinkled at the corners as he wrote in a small notebook. His long white beard nearly dipped into his plate of food, which sat mostly untouched.

How could I get my business to thrive like the bakery? I'd been reading business books all week, but between moving in, taking over the shop, mourning Nana, and settling into town, I felt like I didn't have enough time for anything—like I was stretching myself in too many directions and not succeeding at any of it. Realizing I was biting my nails again, I shoved my hands into my pockets. Comparing my shop to Nancy's was going to stress me out even more than I already was.

A group of teenagers sat together at a table in the middle of the room, their animated chatter filling the air. A girl fiddled with the plaid tablecloth that matched the autumn vibe, and one of the boys juggled three of the miniature pumpkins that had been decorating the tables.

"Don't make me call your mother, Evan," Nancy yelled from behind the counter.

"Sorry, Mrs. Simmon." The boy ducked his head and returned the pumpkins to their rightful spots, his freckles standing out against the blush spreading across his cheeks.

Mine reacted in much the same way whenever I got embarrassed or angry.

In Whisper Hollow, everyone knew everyone. They even remembered me from the summers I visited Nana while growing up, although that had been years ago. A *lot* had changed, but at least Nancy's bakery was familiar. The only thing missing was Nana, who'd spent hours gossiping with Nancy.

The couple in line ahead of me finally made their choice and moved on, leaving me free to move to the counter. A garland of fall leaves in hues of burnt orange, deep red, and golden yellow stretched across it, framing an assortment of delectable pastries and confections displayed in glass containers.

"Back again, I see." Nancy winked and handed over a drink, like she'd been doing every day since I'd moved in.

"Let me pay for this one," I said.

"Don't be silly. You're doing me a favor, helping me test out flavors for new drinks. Today is pumpkin pie hot chocolate." She flashed a smile at me. "Should I assume you'll be having the turkey, apple, brie sandwich?"

"That's right, but so I don't get too predictable, I'll also take one of these." I plucked an apple from the pile of fruit near the counter where Nancy had put some autumn produce on a charming wooden cart adorned with burlap bows.

"There are few things I love more than a predictable customer." Nancy rang up my order before tucking a lock of gray-streaked hair behind her ear.

"Glad to be of service."

She looked around, though I was the last one in line, and lowered her voice. Even her discreet voice was a little too loud. "I heard Marty came by again today."

Marty must be Mr. James's first name. It had only been two hours since his visit, so of course, Nancy already knew about it.

"Yup." I drummed my fingers on the counter, not wanting to revisit the day's unpleasantness.

"He's too big for his britches, walking around like he owns all of Main Street instead of a quarter of it." She tsked and shook her head. "He's way out of line. I swear he's threatened half the owners on our side of the street in the last few days. Someone needs to give him a good talking to." She frowned, deepening the wrinkles on her face.

"I'm not sure a good talking to would do the trick." But it was comforting to know that I wasn't alone. Maybe his hounding was less personal than it felt. Although, I had no idea what he stood to gain from bothering a successful business like Sugarplum Delights.

"Your grandmother sure didn't agree. I heard her give him a good tongue lashing a time or two. Those two went at it often enough." She shook her head with a fond smile that faded. "He was in here earlier, but thankfully Peter shooed him off." She tilted her head toward the older gentleman with the beard, who was taking a break from his notebook to eat his pastry.

"Can he teach me how to do that?" Not that shooing him off would do any good, unless I miraculously found a way to come up with the rent.

Nancy laughed. "It's less to do with what Peter said and more to do with their rivalry. They both own too much of this town, but Peter doesn't flaunt his wealth. From what I remember, the two had a pretty intense disagreement years ago." She leaned close over the counter. "They hate each other."

I looked over my shoulder toward Peter, who took another bite of his pastry.

"But now I've gone and said too much. Me and my silly mouth." Nancy giggled and passed me my food. "Anyway, are you coming to the festival tonight?"

"I'll try to swing by later, but it's my nephew's birthday, and I promised to video chat in for the party." I left the counter, claimed an empty table, and devoured my food while it was still warm.

As I headed toward the door fifteen minutes later, Nancy called out, "Harper, wait!" She bustled over and held out an envelope to me. "This letter was buried under a pile of papers on my desk, and I found it this morning. I promised Bettye I'd give it to you when you took over the shop."

"You mean *if* I took over the shop."

Her eyes twinkled. "Don't be silly, Harper. She always knew you would. No one loved her shop more than you."

I swallowed past the lump in my throat and accepted the letter. Nana's death last month was still too recent. "Thanks, Nancy."

I returned to my table and opened Nana's letter with shaking hands. Finding the letter was like finding a piece of Nana that I didn't know was missing.

My Little Ink-Harp,

I smiled at the nickname. Nana had started calling me that after we read the book *Inkheart* together.

I know the shop is an enormous responsibility and can be stressful at times. But I don't want it to be stressful. I want you to hold on to your childhood memories of this place and keep your love for it. I'm giving you some money that I've been saving over the years in case I ever had the opportunity to buy Whispering Pages and own it outright. (I hope you have better luck getting that miserly Mr. James to sell than I did.)

Love,

Nana

P.S. The money is hidden inside a hollowed-out copy of Inkheart *in my office. I hope your life here can rival any of the stories you'd find within these walls.*

Relief flooded me. If Nana had money saved up, I'd be able to make the rent and keep my childhood haven safe from Mr. James's greedy hands for a little longer.

Following her instructions, I hurried back to Whispering Pages, slipping in through the back door this time since it was closer to the office, and found the copy of *Inkheart* on the bookshelf in her office. I pulled out the book and stroked a finger over the familiar cover, smiling at the memories it evoked. Nana and I had read the entire series together one summer. Another memory of the place I had to—and would be able to—protect. Nana's money would fix everything.

I wiped away a tear and opened the book. My eyes widened as I took in its contents—or rather, lack of contents. The only thing resting inside the book was a scrap of paper.

Nana's money was gone.

Chapter 2

A Murder of Crows

I woke to Jiji jumping on my chest. After pushing her off with a muttered curse, I snuggled deeper into Nana's patchwork quilt. I'd been up way too late searching the house for Nana's missing money in case she'd forgotten to put it in *Inkheart* like she'd said.

Jiji thrust her wet nose in my ear.

I sat up and glared at her, but I couldn't resist petting her fuzzy head. "Is that necessary?"

She meowed and tilted her head to the side. If I tried to ignore her like I had the first few days, she'd inevitably get into some sort of mischief. So far, she'd eaten—and thrown up—plastic bags, meowed incessantly, kneaded her claws on my back while I tried to sleep, and sat directly on my face.

I got up to feed her with a resigned sigh, then changed into leggings and a long-sleeved T-shirt. There'd be no going back to sleep now, and a run would help clear my head.

Out on the porch, I stumbled over a bag sitting in front of the door. When I opened it, I found a copy of *The Silmarillion* with a printed receipt from Whispering Pages inside the front cover. I looked around, but I was alone. Who would've dropped such a thing off at my place, and why?

With a shrug, I put it on my kitchen table to take to work with me and left for my run. My alabaster cottage, with its sagging porch and red-shuttered windows, sat by itself in the woods. My closest neighbor was a mile away—giving me access to about a hundred different running paths that I'd reacquainted myself with throughout the last week. I shivered in the crisp morning air and ran a little faster to get my blood pumping. The forest floor crunched under my feet, and the first hint of daylight lit the eastern sky with a faint pink tinge.

Grace didn't like it when I went running in the woods by myself, but what did she expect me to do when I lived alone? At least I was running in the morning instead of at night. She hated it when I ran at night. But honestly, I lived in Whisper Hollow now, not Phoenix. The worst I had to fear was black bears, which was why I ran with pepper spray. Not as good as bear spray, but better than nothing.

My mind worked best while my body was in motion, and I needed to figure out what I was going to do about the rent.

But first came the task of figuring out who took Nana's money. How could I find it? For now, I'd talk to the sheriff and Nancy. Maybe she would recognize the stenciled floral design I'd found on the backside of the paper in *Inkheart*.

The sound of my breathing blended with the steady rhythm of my footsteps and matched with the forest's heartbeat. Each inhale brought me closer to nature—the earthy scent of fallen leaves, pine trees, and rich soil—and each exhale helped release my tension. I passed under a copse of oak trees, their red and gold leaves casting dappled sunlight on the dew-kissed trail under my feet.

A branch cracked behind me, and I whipped my head around and slowed. Aside from the trees and dirt path, nothing seemed out of the ordinary, yet my heart pounded. I pulled the pepper spray from my pocket and kept running.

Maybe I wasn't alone.

As I rounded a bend, a burst of caws and flapping wings shattered the forest's muted breath. I skidded to a stop and barely kept myself from screaming. The birds flew overhead, their glossy black plumage and sharp beaks identifying them as a murder of crows.

I laughed at my ridiculousness even as my pulse still raced. Of course I wasn't alone. I was surrounded by animals, which was probably what had made the noise behind me.

Another twig snapped. Weren't animals supposed to be quieter?

I hushed my gasping breaths, my gaze darting around the forest. Thankfully, it was bright now, but the surrounding trees obscured my view and cast long, menacing shadows.

Behind me, a shape darted between the heavy foliage and in and out of sight on the winding path. Something tall and running on two feet. Something distinctly human.

Heart pounding, I spun around and took off. Maybe it was someone out for a run. But maybe it wasn't. I didn't want to find out. My thoughts scrambled to the book on my porch. I'd thought it was harmless, but someone had been near my house earlier that morning.

My hand tightened around my pepper spray. The small canister felt wholly inadequate against my rising panic. Every snap of a twig sent shivers down my spine. I imagined the person behind me getting closer and closer. The trees closed in around me, their branches reaching for me like outstretched arms trying to catch me while the roots tried to trip me.

"Hey!" a deep voice behind me yelled.

The shout made the hairs on my neck stand on end, and my skin prickled. I pushed myself faster. My breaths came in ragged gasps. Fear and adrenaline fueled my footsteps despite the burning in my legs.

"Stop!" The voice was closer now, practically right behind me.

I sprinted as fast as I could.

The crow's dark silhouettes wove through the forest canopy around me.

A heavy hand fell on my shoulder. "You dropped—"

I whirled around and released a stream of pepper spray at my attacker.

The man knocked my hand away, dropping something to the ground with a clatter as he raised both hands to his face, which was hidden under the hood of his jacket.

I turned to run, but my gaze caught the shiny object lying among the carpet of leaves. A cell phone. *My* cell phone. "H-how did you know that was mine?" My words came out in a rush that mirrored my racing heart. There was still enough residue in the air that my eyes stung, but I held the pepper spray in front of me.

"You were the only one"—he coughed—"out here."

"Oh." I stared at it as my terror morphed into surprise and then embarrassment at about the same speed that my heart was pounding. I picked up my phone and dropped it into the small pocket of my leggings, my flaming cheeks making it difficult to meet his gaze. "Well, thank you."

The man staggered to the side to lean against a tree. Now that he wasn't chasing me, he looked much less like a predator and much more like a man out for his morning run. He sounded like he was around my age, but without seeing his face, it was hard to know for sure.

As I followed him into uncontaminated air, it grew easier to breathe. "I'm sorry for spraying you. Are you okay?"

"Of course I'm not okay. You pepper sprayed me"—a fit of coughing interrupted him—"in the face. Are you crazy?"

My cheeks heated. Okay, so maybe I'd been a little trigger-happy, but it wasn't all my fault. "I'm sorry. You scared me. You should've called out to me."

"I tried," he mumbled.

Now that he mentioned it, he had started to say something before I sprayed him. Maybe it was my fault for freaking out.

"Can I do anything?" I touched his forearm.

"You've done enough." He shrugged me off and started to stagger down the path.

"Wait!" I grabbed him. "At least take off your hoodie."

"What?" His eyes widened, but then he squeezed them shut again.

"I don't mean like *that*." My cheeks heated for the millionth time. It'd be great if they could stop doing that. "I'm pretty sure you should remove clothing that has been affected. And don't touch your face," I added as he reached up to rub at his eyes.

"Fine." He yanked off his hoodie, and I bit my lip as the move exposed a strip of muscled stomach before he pulled his T-shirt down to cover it.

Unfortunately, his face was just as appealing, aside from the red, watery eyes. He had a strong jaw with a well-groomed beard that accentuated the contours of his face. He looked like a sexy cross between Aragorn and Christian Bale, a dangerous combination. Plus, he had the kind of dark chestnut hair that made me want to run my fingers through it.

"This *would* happen on my morning run. What were you thinking, pepper spraying me?"

His obvious dislike squashed my rising admiration just in time. I didn't need a distraction like him in my life. I crossed my arms across my chest. "Maybe next time you should call out to a woman *before* you chase her down in a secluded forest."

"No good deed goes unpunished," he muttered.

"Not when you do it like that."

We glared at each other until his eyes watered again.

"You need to rinse out your eyes."

"I'll do it at home." He stalked down the path without looking back.

Heart still pounding, I stared after his retreating figure. If I was lucky, I'd never see the guy again, so I wouldn't have to untangle my feelings about him. Though, considering how small Whisper Hollow was, odds were I *would* see him. At least I could refrain from pepper spraying him from now on. Our next meeting was bound to be less terrible.

I sighed and finished my run before heading home. By the time I was ready for work, my heart rate had returned to normal. I collected the mysterious book I'd found on my porch and put it in my bike basket next to Jiji, who had an uncanny sense for when I was heading to the shop. Nana once told me she'd gotten in the habit of taking Jiji to Whispering Pages with her, but it was still strange to me. The cat blinked at me, and her tail twitched as I wheeled the bike off the porch to ride to town. Did normal cats ride in bike baskets, or was it a Jiji thing?

After I huffed and puffed my way up the huge hill—getting off my bike to push it part way—I made it to the outskirts of town. Sprawling ranch-style homes dotted the sidewalks until they shifted to charming colonial-style houses farther in.

Fifteen minutes later, I coasted down Main Street, where towering trees decorated either side of the street. A faint breeze rustled their limbs, sending occasional orange showers drifting around me like confetti. Outside of Main Street Makers–one of the best-decorated shops in town–artfully arranged bales of hay sat on either side of the front doors with an assortment of pumpkins, gourds, and squashes. An autumn wreath hung on the door, its crimson and amber ribbons dancing in the wind.

Strangely enough, Sugarplum Delights wasn't open yet. Maybe Nancy was taking Saturday morning off after the festival. I needed to call to make sure everything was okay.

At Whispering Pages, I locked up my bike, and Jiji hopped out of the basket. I glanced at the display window as I retrieved my key, then looked again. The skeleton that should've been reaching into the cauldron of candy was gone. Maybe it had fallen over or Kyle had moved him somewhere and I hadn't noticed.

A folded piece of paper rested on the ground near the front door. I picked it up, thinking it was trash, but my name caught my eye. Unfolding it, I read the messy scrawl.

If you end the lease early, I'll cancel the early termination clause, and I'll make sure you get your grandmother's full deposit back.

-Marty James

Was he trying to bribe me now? Why was he so desperate?

I shoved the note in my pocket and opened the door. The bell's cheery jingle felt almost mocking in the ensuing silence. A pungent smell clung to the air along with a sense of wrongness.

A half-collapsed display table lay at an awkward angle, one of the legs broken. A decorative cobweb hung across a few rogue pumpkins like a shroud, fluttering faintly in the draft from the door. It was like some bad Halloween prank gone wrong.

I stepped closer to examine the mess, and the floor creaked under me. The sound amplified the thud of my heart. The tablecloth that had been pulled from a display covered a body-shaped lump on the floor. How had the skeleton gotten covered up like that? Had Kyle come back in after I'd locked up, or had someone broken in?

The heater turned on like it always did then, and the fallen table-cloth fluttered. I stepped forward, and my shoe made a small suction sound. The floor was sticky, like someone had spilled soda. The shop had been pristine before I'd left the night before. Well, as pristine as the tiny little bookshop ever was.

My stomach clenched with dread. Something was wrong. My shoes squelched as I approached the collapsed table, and I reached toward the tablecloth with a trembling hand.

The door jingled as someone came in. "Hey, Harper."

I whirled around to face Kyle, my heart jumping to my throat. "You scared me. You aren't scheduled to come in until later."

"I wanted to ask about extra hours for next week." He took in the mess behind me, his brow furrowing. "What happened?"

"I don't know. Looks like someone vandalized the place. I'll call the police." My gaze fell on the skeleton that had collapsed into a pile of bones by the front window. If the skeleton was there, then what was under . . .

Turning back around, I slowly reached for the tablecloth. I pulled it free and screamed as I stared down at Mr. James's lifeless body lying in a pool of blood.

Chapter 3

The Dead Keep Their Secrets

"Do you have any idea how a dead body ended up in your shop, Miss Coleman?" Sheriff Warner leaned forward in the chair facing my office desk, which I sat behind. He laced his fingers together, resting his elbows on his knees. His leather jacket creaked at the movement, and his hat somewhat hid the graying hair at his temples and shaded his brown eyes.

"No." At the thought of Mr. James, his face flashed through my mind again, and I shivered. How could someone have been in my shop without me knowing? Was I even safe there? "But I wonder if this is related to my grandmother's missing money."

"Missing money?"

"Yes." I took a moment to fill him in, even passing him Nana's note, then continued. "I was going to report it last night, but I wanted to make sure it wasn't somewhere at home first. But now, with finding the body this morning, it seems too coincidental not to be related, don't you think?"

"It is suspicious." The letter crinkled in his hand as he skimmed it again before setting it down on my desk next to a stack of books. "Do you know how much it was?"

"Um, no, but I think it was a significant amount." I stared out my office's glass door at the crime scene techs wearing coveralls and gloves as they moved around the shop, took pictures, and collected evidence—at least that was what I assumed, based on the murder mystery shows Grace and Nana watched during our summer visits. "Maybe Mr. James took the money and someone killed him for it?" I tried to put the pieces together. It felt like all the answers were within reach but too fuzzy to discern. How odd that I'd woken up to one world—a world where life was safe and normal—and now I was living in one where there was a dead body in my bookshop.

"There's not a lot I can do about missing money when I'm not confident it was there in the first place or how much it was, so for now, I'll focus on the death." Sheriff Warner frowned and pulled out a notebook that looked as weathered as he did and flipped to a page. His gaze flicked over whatever was written there, then darted to me. "According to your employee, Mr. James has been in a few times since you took over the shop, and you had quite a few disagreements"—he lingered on the word *disagreements*—"about what to do with the place."

I couldn't help but glance toward the second floor where Kyle had spent the last fifteen minutes talking to the sheriff. What else had he told him? How he'd walked in and found me standing over the dead body?

"Yes, we had, but I didn't kill him. I couldn't do something like that." I pulled my feet under me. A man had requested my shoes after discovering I'd stepped in Mr. James's blood.

Sheriff Warner frowned, and the movement wrinkled his bushy gray mustache. "Mr. Sánchez reported overhearing you say something about killing someone yesterday."

"I never said anything like that!" My voice shook, and I swallowed again, trying to ease the growing tightness in my throat.

"Something about killing someone named Tate?" he read from his notebook.

"That was me ranting to my sister about my ex-boyfriend. I wouldn't kill anyone." I blew out an exasperated breath and kept myself from mentioning that it was Grace who was supposed to kill him anyway. Darn Kyle and his big mouth.

"Can I get her contact information?"

I gave him Grace's cell number, then sucked in a slow breath to try to calm my pounding heart. "Okay, I know how this looks, but I promise I didn't kill Mr. James. I don't even know how he died. The last time I saw him was when he came in to talk about my lease yesterday. I told him I'd get him the money and that I wasn't going to end the lease early. But that's it. I stopped by Nancy's after closing up, then I went home and video-chatted with my nephew for his birthday, and read *Austenland* until I fell asleep on the couch." I took a few deep breaths to calm my pounding heart and blinked to push back the tears threatening to rise.

Sheriff Warner scribbled something else in his notebook, and I glimpsed the word *motive* upside down.

"I think I need a lawyer." I stopped chewing on my nails and readjusted the blanket an officer had given me. I should really stop fidgeting. It was probably making me look nervous and guilty. I shoved my hand under my leg.

Even the skeleton, still collapsed on the floor by the front window, stared at me with empty, accusing eye sockets. If only I could ask him what had happened.

"We're only asking questions, not pressing charges. We still have quite a few things to look into." He snapped his notebook shut, but an unspoken *yet* hovered between us. He opened my office door and waved me out. "I'll see what I can find out about your grandmother's missing money as well."

Through the shop's glass windows, a few curious onlookers peered inside. My stomach shriveled even more. Great. Once word of this got out, Whispering Pages would lose what little revenue it had. No one would want to frequent a bookshop where a murder had happened—especially not if they thought the owner was the murderer. Even for Halloween, that was probably a bit too macabre.

Jiji sprang from a bookshelf where she'd been hiding and landed on my shoulder. I gasped and held a hand to my heart. "Sorry. I guess I'm a little on edge." I ran a trembling hand down Jiji's head. She purred and watched me with large, unblinking eyes.

"Get this cat out of here," Sheriff Warner barked. "We can't have an animal contaminating the crime scene."

Another officer with dark hair and a thin nose approached. He reached for Jiji, and she leaped off my shoulder with a loud yowl.

"Let me get her." I padded after her, careful to navigate around the blood. My socks were near-silent on the wood floor.

Jiji stopped near a science-fiction shelf, not too far from where I'd discovered Mr. James's body. She sniffed at something under the shelf, then meowed.

"Come on, Jiji. You have to go." I picked her up, but she wiggled free and jumped to the floor. She meowed again, not looking away from the shelf.

"What is it?" If I had to deal with mice in the shop after everything else, I was going to lose it. I knelt next to Jiji and shined my phone's flashlight under the shelf, ignoring the way the sheriff loomed behind me. The light glinted off something shiny, and my stomach dropped. "There's something here."

"Let me see." The dark-haired officer joined me on the ground and reached under the shelf with a gloved hand. He pulled out a hammer with dried blood covering the flat end.

"Looks like we've found our murder weapon," Sheriff Warner said.

A tech wearing a pair of gloves approached with a camera. My heart sped up to match the *click, click, click* as he took picture after picture.

I stared at the gray lines running up the hammer's blue handle. "That isn't mine. Like I said, I went to Nancy's after closing up the shop—she can vouch for me there—and my sister can vouch for me during the party."

"And what time would you say you got off the phone?"

"Around eight." My voice came out too small.

"And you live alone?"

"Y-yes."

"We've been informed that the approximate time of death was between nine and midnight last night. Can anyone verify your whereabouts during that time?"

My heart sank. "No." Even as a whisper, the words barely made it out through the tightness in my throat.

He made another thoughtful noise that seemed to say, *Things aren't looking too good.*

"You've got to believe me. I'm as confused as you are by all of this." My heart thumped painfully in my chest, and I held the blanket tighter to hide my shaking hands. Why had Nana never invested in security cameras? "If you arrest me, that means the real killer will still be out there."

Sheriff Warner wrote something else in his book. "We'll continue to look into things. If you think of anything else that might be important, let me know."

Head spinning with questions, I followed him to the door. How had Mr. James gotten inside? What was going to happen to the bookstore now? And most importantly, who killed him?

I had to leave to give the police time to work. I slipped outside with Jiji, and she jumped from my arms and took off down the sidewalk. Someone came out of the shop next door, but I averted my gaze, staring at Sugarplum Delights. Was one of Nancy's delicious drinks worth facing a second interrogation? A tug near my waist drew my attention. The yarn of my sweater unraveled along the hem, and I'd already lost a good chunk of the bottom, revealing a sliver of my stomach.

What the—?

I grabbed the yarn, and a pained yowl sounded from the shop next door. It must've been caught on Jiji's collar. Had she somehow slipped inside Grain and Glass? The yarn slipped from my fingers, but instead of grabbing it again and risking hurting Jiji, I dashed toward the shop, holding my arms over my stomach while more of my sweater unraveled.

The mingled scents of sawdust and varnish hit me as I darted between a beautifully carved wooden table on one side and a display of gorgeous glass-blown decorations. Thank goodness the shop was empty so no one could see me so out of sorts.

The yarn led me through the shop like a dreaded string of fate that connected me to the stinking cat.

A shout and a crash came from a back room—the same place Jiji's string led.

"Oh no." I ran through the door, which was propped open, gathering the loose thread as I went.

A tall figure coated in sawdust stood by a half-finished rocking chair, holding a very pleased-looking Jiji away from his body. He lowered the cat, giving me a glimpse of his face.

The man from the forest.

Who happened to be the owner of the other shop next to mine. Of course he was, because life loved to throw plot twists at me.

"You again."

"I'm so sorry." I grabbed a rag off a workbench and held it out to the sawdust-covered man. Hopefully, it wasn't Jiji's fault he was a mess, but with my luck, it would be.

My thoughts darted to the body in my shop next door. Was it too much of a coincidence that Jiji had found the murder weapon and then led me straight to this man? Or was it just bad timing?

"Is this little terror yours?" The man clenched his jaw and eyed the yarn connecting Jiji to me. He passed her over with a muscled arm and accepted the rag.

"Jiji isn't a terror," I said indignantly, even as she wiggled from my arms and dropped to the ground to wind around his ankles. "Just a traitor."

"My broken shelf would say otherwise." He wiped his face clean, but sawdust still covered his hair, dark-gray tee, and blue jeans.

"Are you okay?" I asked.

"No, I'm not. Thanks to your cat, I'm now behind schedule for a really big order." He shifted his scowl from the mess beside him to Jiji, his eyes still a little red.

A faint blush heated my cheeks. "You don't need to be so rude about it. I already apologized." Why were the attractive ones always jerks?

"Your apology isn't going to fix this mess." He ran a hand through his already tousled hair, raining sawdust onto his broad shoulders. "This is the last thing I needed today."

That made two of us.

"You shouldn't bring your cat to town if you can't control her." He sneezed. "Get that furball out of here. I can't afford any more delays."

"Sorry we ruined your day."

It was no wonder I wasn't in any rush to get back to dating after Tate, with men like this guy out there. I tried to scoop up Jiji. She evaded my hands and bolted between my legs, twisting the yarn around me. "Jiji, stop."

I turned to grab her at the same moment the man moved, and the yarn around our ankles caught, binding us together as if we were in a three-legged race. The taut yarn snapped, and we crashed to the ground in a tangle of limbs.

His weight landed on me, and my breath whooshed from my lungs. Our faces were way too close, and my heart took off. A shiver ran through me at his proximity. The man's dark-blue gaze met mine, and his eyes widened. I inhaled sharply, taking in his cedar scent.

I'd come to Whisper Hollow to get away from men, not closer to them. And whether I was talking about looks or the potential for getting me in trouble, this sexy stalker, who may or may not be connected to the murder, was an eleven out of ten.

Chapter 4

Night and Day

The man shifted to the side, and Jiji leaped from his back. "What were you saying about her not being a terror?"

"I guess I underestimated her." I climbed to my feet and snagged Jiji, the loose yarn trailing behind me. "Sorry about your project," I said over my shoulder, albeit grudgingly. With one hand holding tight to the wriggling Jiji, I shoved the door and hit something hard.

"Ow." The voice came from the other side of the door, then someone pulled it the rest of the way open.

"Are you okay?" I asked the man rubbing his forehead. He had the same smoldering eyes, chiseled jaw, and angular features as the guy behind me, lending them both an air of mystery, but his hair was a little lighter and hung to his ears in slight waves.

The resemblance was too strong for them to be anything but brothers. But where the guy behind me had broader shoulders and stockier arms, his brother had a lean, athletic build. What was in the water in this town? Or maybe it ran in their family.

"And who are you?" The man's gaze dipped down to my middle, and he looked up with an amused smile that revealed even white teeth.

I flushed at what I looked like right then and held Jiji in front of my exposed stomach. "I'm . . . just leaving," I mumbled without meeting his gaze.

"That's too bad. It isn't often we have a pretty woman in our workshop." He flashed that grin again, revealing a single dimple obscured by his neatly trimmed beard. He also didn't move out of my way.

"Probably for good reason." I tried and failed to resist looking at the mess behind me.

The man followed my gaze to his sawdust-covered brother, then to my mess of a sweater and the wriggling cat in my arms. He barked out a laugh. "It seems I missed quite a bit."

"Don't distract her, Coop," Mr. Sexy Stalker said.

"Maybe I *want* to distract her."

My cheeks heated for a different reason. Except, I wasn't looking for anyone to flirt with. Especially not when I was about to lose my shirt.

"You'll have to excuse my older brother. He gets a little stressed about deadlines, work, people, and, well, lots of things really. When you throw a beautiful woman into the mix"—the new brother threw his hands into the air and flashed another easy smile at me—"I'm sure you can tell why I'm usually the one who deals with the customers."

I couldn't help but return his smile with a small one of my own. Some of the tension eased from my shoulders. "Thank you, but I should get going. I didn't mean to interrupt."

"Please, feel free to interrupt anytime," the younger brother said. "I'm Cooper, by the way, but my friends call me Coop. And that's my brother Seb."

"It's Sebastian," the other brother called crankily.

So my sexy stalker had a name.

"I'm Harper." Only Grace called me Harp, because I sucked at making friends. And first impressions, apparently. I could add it to my growing list of failures. I shook Cooper's hand while trying to maintain my death grip on Jiji, who yowled in annoyance and clawed at my arm. No way was she getting free in this shop again.

"Cute cat," Cooper said.

"Thanks."

Jiji put her nose in the air, not interested in being nice to anyone who actually liked cats.

"It was nice to meet you." At least it was nice to meet one of them, anyway.

"You too. I hope to see you again soon." Cooper opened the door with a gallant bow.

I giggled and stepped outside. He was ridiculous, but at least he was more fun than his brother. One brought fun to a situation and the other sucked it out like a thirsty vampire. "You probably will."

When Cooper's smile widened, I realized my comment came out flirtier than I'd intended. We'd see each other again since our shops were neighbors, but considering the strange first impression I'd definitely given, I didn't want to reveal that I owned Whispering Pages.

"Because I'll be around." My cheeks were still too warm. "Anyway, bye." I hurried down the sidewalk.

Jiji let out a plaintive yowl, and I glared at her. "I hope you're happy. That was extremely embarrassing, and you could not have worse taste in guys." We had that in common. "Those two brothers are about as opposite as night and day, and of course, you had to go and make a terrible first impression."

For a moment, I couldn't help but reflect on Sebastian's grumpy expression and Cooper's easy smile. What made them so different? At least they didn't know I worked next door.

I shook my head and pushed them from my thoughts. I didn't need to be thinking of men right now. My heart twinged as I remembered

Tate, and I shoved him away too. I had bigger issues, like trying to figure out how to clear my name and pay the rent. I gathered my things and biked home, putting Jiji in the basket and my AirPod in my ear.

"You won't believe what happened," I said to Grace as I biked down Main Street.

"You fell madly in love with a customer and had a shotgun wedding?"

"Wow. Your ability is uncanny. How do you do that every time?"

Grace laughed. "All right, Miss Sarcasm. What happened?"

Two women pushing strollers on the sidewalk looked at me and whispered to one another. With the police cars that had been parked outside all morning, word had spread about what had happened. And if Nancy was any indication, this town loved to gossip.

I biked a little faster and changed what I was going to say. Rather than jumping into the dead body while still biking home where anyone could overhear, I started with the embarrassing story about Jiji. "Jiji's collar caught on my sweater and half-unraveled it. And I had to chase her next door, where I ran into two guys. Then Jiji messed up one of their projects for work, and it was so embarrassing."

"What two guys?"

"Sebastian and Cooper."

Overhead, the branches cast shadows that danced across the sidewalk ahead of me.

"Oh yeah. I remember Nana mentioning them once or twice. They own the woodworking shop?"

"Nana talked about them?" I coasted down the hill that caused me so much trouble in the mornings. I was determined to make it up the hill without stopping by the end of the month.

"Yeah, she loved them," Grace's voice pulled me back to the present. "They helped her with all sorts of projects, and she'd feed them dinner all the time. I guess they moved to town a few years ago and she took them under her wing."

"That sounds like Nana."

"You were too distracted by Tate the Lying Cheater to pay attention when Nana talked about them," she said, "but she wanted you to date one of them. I could tell. Jeff and I are all for it too."

My chest clenched at the mention of Tate, though I couldn't help but smile at her nickname for him. "Nana wanted me to date Cooper?"

Jiji gave me a judgmental look. Actually, that was her normal face.

"Hmm . . . I think it was the other one—the older brother."

"Sebastian?" I snorted. "That'll never happen." I'd try to rescue Nana's shop, but I draw the line at taking dating recommendations from her. Absolutely no dating. Letting people in was the same as letting them hurt you—a lesson I'd learned all too well. "Guys can*not* be trusted."

"Harp, you can't judge everyone like that because of Tate the Lying Cheater."

"I can and I will."

"Fine. You don't need to date anyone." Grace sighed.

I could imagine the way she'd tug at the ends of her long, mahogany hair. The thought had me running a hand through my similarly-colored curls, which stopped at my shoulders and was still shorter than I was used to thanks to the haircut I'd gotten after Tate.

"No harm in a little flirting though, right?"

"There's something else I need to tell you." I changed the subject none too subtly. Talking about a dead body was still better than talking about my dating life. I locked my bike up on Nana's wraparound porch with shaking hands, trying not to think of Mr. James's still form.

"Well, what is it? Is Mr. James bothering you again?" Her voice took on a sharp edge like it did when she got anxious.

"Not in the way you're thinking."

The scent of cinnamon and spiced apple greeted me as I stepped through the front door, thanks to the air freshener I'd plugged into the hall. The familiar scent drew some of the tension from my shoulders. With Nana's orange and yellow plaid throw pillows on the couch, it was sort of like being hugged by fall—or by Nana—every time I came home, which was exactly what I needed right now. If only she were here to give me advice. Tears pricked at my eyes, but I dashed them away.

"Mr. James is dead," I said at the same time a crashing noise came from Grace's end, then a muffled shout sounded from her kids.

Based on the sass, I'd say it was seven-year-old Lexi.

A chill wind cut through the area, rustling the trees around the house, and I shivered. Even in the bright afternoon sunlight, the woods were full of shadows. Somewhere in this small, supposedly peaceful town, a murderer walked loose.

Jiji hopped from the bike and wove between my legs. The traitorous cat. Finding that murder weapon and then acting like she'd done nothing wrong.

"What did you say? Sorry, I couldn't hear over the kids arguing."

"I said Mr. James is dead," I repeated louder now that I was in the safety of my house.

"What?" she screeched, and I held the phone away from my ear. "How? What happened?"

"I don't know, but I found his body in the shop this morning—"

"In the shop?" she said shrilly. "What's going on?"

I spent the next half hour filling her in on everything that had happened, including Nana's missing money and how they were probably going to call her as well. While we talked, I paced from the living room to the kitchen and back, tripping over the wooden chair by the kitchen table. A pumpkin-shaped ceramic bowl held a mix of fruit, and I devoured a pear while working my way through the story.

"I can't believe this happened at the same time as Nana's missing money," she said after I finished.

"You're telling me." I collapsed onto the crimson sofa sitting against the wall under a large semicircular window. Now that I'd finished telling her the story, my nervous energy dissipated.

"I hope you didn't say anything without a lawyer."

"The sheriff said I didn't need one since he wasn't charging me with anything." Not yet, anyway.

Grace sighed. "Harp, you always need a lawyer. Didn't you pay any attention to those murder mysteries?"

"You mean the ones you two watched while I read my books?"

"That's it. I'm coming to see you." A door slammed in the background, as if she were heading outside.

"You can't pull the kids out of school, and Jeff won't be back from drill until the end of next week."

She groaned but said nothing more.

"I'll be all right. Obviously, I didn't do it, so I need to convince the police of that." I pulled the knitted cream throw from the back of the couch over me and burrowed into its warm embrace.

"And how will you do that?" she said. "Not that they should need it, considering you're like five-five and not even a hundred and twenty pounds. Plus, if you say that you need to convince them, it makes it sound like you're guilty."

"Whatever. The point is, I don't have an alibi. The easiest way to clear my name is to figure out who killed him." Needing something to do with my hands, I re-situated the gourd, miniature pumpkin, and dried corn on the cob sitting on the coffee table.

"Yes, that sounds like the *easiest* way."

"Okay, maybe *easy* wasn't the best word choice, but it would be the surest way of proving my innocence," I said.

"I don't like the idea of you tracking down a murderer. You should leave it to the police."

"I won't do anything crazy," I said. "I'm only going to look into things a bit. He was found in *my* shop, Grace, and not even twelve hours after I discovered Nana's missing money."

I sighed and returned the gourd to its spot, then shoved a handful of the candy corn from a bowl on the coffee table into my mouth. A symphony of marshmallow, vanilla, and honey flavors burst to life with each bite. I'd already had to refill the bowl once since moving in last week. Stress eating and candy decorations weren't a good combination.

"I hate the thought of you doing this alone."

"I'll be okay. I just need to figure out my next step."

"Do you think this is related to Nana's missing money?" she asked.

"I don't know, but the timing seems too coincidental not to be."

Grace swore under her breath, and in the background a kid yelled, "Mommy owes money to the swear jar!"

"Really, Grace, don't worry about me," I said. She didn't need to know how freaked out I was.

"How can I not worry about you when you're by yourself? Probably sitting at home alone biting your nails like you always do when you're stressed."

Guiltily, I pulled my hand from my mouth again.

"I wish none of this had happened," she said with a sigh.

"So does everyone who lives during such times, but that's not for them to decide. All we can decide is what to do with our time."

"Why do you sound like you're quoting Dumbledore?"

"Close. That was Gandalf, though I might have butchered it." I walked to my bookshelf and ran a hand over the worn spines. For all the adventures I'd read, I'd never thought to end up in one. "You said part of the quote, and I had to finish it."

"How was that close? One's from *Harry Potter* and the other is from *Lord of the Flies*."

I sighed, though I couldn't help but crack a smile. "It's *Lord of the Rings*, Grace. And I said you were close because at least Dumbledore and Gandalf are both wizards."

"Well, if you're speaking nerd again, you aren't doing too bad." Grace's voice was still heavy with worry. "They can't seriously believe it was you, though. How would you even take someone out?"

"With a hammer, evidently." I turned to stare out the window and pulled the sheer curtains closed. I ran a finger over the intricate stitching of autumn leaves—another reminder of Nana and how alone I was.

"He was killed by a hammer?" Grace lowered her voice on the word *killed*, probably because a kid was nearby. "What else do you know?"

"He was killed sometime between nine and midnight."

"During the festival you skipped?"

I groaned. "Don't rub it in. I'm already painfully aware that I wouldn't be in this predicament had I made myself leave the house after Logan's party."

Grace tactfully avoided saying anything else about it, like how she'd encouraged me to go. "Can you think of anyone else who might've done this?"

"Um . . ." I thought about the people I'd met over the last week, then gasped. "Nancy."

"You think Nosy Nancy killed Mr. James?"

I almost laughed at the absurdity of the suggestion. How could sweet Nancy, who resembled the cream puffs she was so adept at making, hurt anyone? "No, I think Nancy could help me figure it out. She's always in everyone's business, and last night she pointed out an older gentleman in her shop who hates Mr. James. But I don't know where he lives or works, and since Nancy's shop was closed this morning and I don't know where she lives, I can't ask her yet."

"If you think he's the killer, I'm not sure that I want you asking him anything anyway."

Outside, the wind whistled shrilly, and a few branches scraped against the side of the house like claws trying to get inside. I jumped at the scratch of wood on wood and pushed away the unwelcome image.

"I have to do something, Grace. I can't continue on like nothing happened." I tried to imagine going back to work like normal. Or coming home and reading my books at night as if nothing happened.

"But it could be dangerous, Harp."

I tightened my grip on the phone and swallowed back my fear. "I need to figure out how to get the shop cleaned because apparently the police don't do it for me, but after that, I'll head to Sugarplum Delights. I have to find out what Nancy knows about Peter and Mr. James, the scrap of paper I found inside *Inkheart,* and whether she noticed anything strange at last night's festival."

"Be careful," she said.

"I will." I had no choice if I didn't want to end up like Mr. James.

Chapter 5

Yellow Carnations Mean Disappointment

The next day crawled by as the police finally finished everything they needed to do at my shop so I could hire someone to come clean it. Before leaving my house the following morning, I put on a warm coat to counter the fall chill and pulled my hood up to cover my face. With Jiji nowhere to be found, I rode into town alone. I had to hop off and walk my bike up the hill, but I made it a little farther than usual.

To keep my mind from wandering back to the horrific events of the last two days, I formulated a plan. First things first, I needed one of Nancy's caramel apple ciders to start my morning, then I had to determine Peter's relationship with Mr. James and ask Nancy about the scrap of paper and the festival.

Twenty minutes later, I was a combination of frozen fingers and sweaty armpits as I locked up my bike in the alley flanked by aged brick buildings.

I glanced at Whispering Pages from the corner of my eye, but I couldn't bring myself to go inside. Not yet. Instead, I walk toward Sugarplum Delights with my head down to avoid making eye contact with anyone. I pushed open the glass door, and it collided with someone.

"I'm so sorry. Are you oka—"

Cooper rubbed his nose and gave me a rueful smile. "We really should stop meeting like this."

I flushed. "I didn't even see you there."

"That's all right." Cooper flashed me a teasing smile. "I need someone to keep me on my toes."

"And I need someone to remind me to look where I'm going." Thank goodness Sebastian wasn't around to see me embarrass myself yet again.

"It would seem we make quite a good team, no?" When he smiled like that, it made his whole face light up—unlike grumpy Sebastian. "And every good team uses nicknames."

I laughed and stepped the rest of the way through the door to escape the cold. "Like what?"

"Mario and Luigi."

"Those are their real names."

His brow furrowed, then he snapped his fingers. "Han Solo and Chewbacca."

"I guess they called him Chewy sometimes," I said.

"How about I call you Harpy?"

"Probably not." I grimaced at the thought of the mythical harpies. "But my sister calls me Harp."

He shook his head. "I can't use that if I didn't come up with it. I'll keep brainstorming."

"Good luck with that." I stepped around him and started to make my way to the counter, but his gentle touch on my arm stopped me.

"I heard about what happened."

I turned to look at him. "I suppose you and half the town have heard the gossip by now."

"Well, with everyone coming in for Nancy's delicious treats, how could we not?" He held up a bag filled with baked goods. "I'll fill you in on a little secret about this town."

Would it have something to do with the murder or the missing money?

He leaned close, and I couldn't help but mimic his body language. His warmth washed over me from his proximity. "They say this place is called Whisper Hollow because no one can keep a secret worth crap. News spreads around here faster than wildfire on a dry summer day."

I laughed. "Now you sound like Nancy."

He straightened and gave me another teasing grin. "But seriously, you should've told me you were the new owner of Whispering Pages. I had no idea you were Bettye's granddaughter."

Well, not *quite* the owner, which is what got me into this mess. "Yeah, sorry."

"Oh, don't apologize. I didn't mean it like that. I just meant that I wish I'd known." He ran a hand through his wavy hair. He always seemed to be in motion, as if he couldn't handle the thought of standing still. "Bettye mentioned you a lot, and I wish I'd realized who you were sooner. She took care of me when we moved to this town, ya know? It sucked that we had to miss her funeral. She was like a grandmother to us."

"So that sort of makes us like cousins," I said, then regretted it.

Cooper raised one dark eyebrow in a move I envied. "Cousins?"

"I mean, not in the familial sort of way, but in a small town we're-all-family sort of way." I bit my lip to stop myself from talking anymore.

"Yeah . . . that didn't help at all."

"It didn't, did it?"

"I'm sorry about Bettye's passing," Cooper said. "She was a good lady."

"Thank you." For whatever reason, Nana hadn't told us about her cancer. If she had, I would've made more of an effort to visit.

"I better get going. Seb doesn't like it when I keep him waiting." Cooper gave a ridiculous little bow, then headed out the door.

I stared after him. Anything beyond friendship was out of the question, but *maybe* I could be friends with Cooper. He seemed like a good guy—unlike his moody brother.

"Well, who needs Korean dramas when you're in here steaming up my shop like that?" Nancy called over the counter with a wink. Thankfully, the shop wasn't too full at the moment.

"There are so many things to address in that statement that I'm not even sure where to begin." I blushed and walked over to the counter. The sight of the pumpkin-shaped cookies frosted with smiling jack-o'-lantern faces and loaves of spiced bread with swirls of cinnamon and cream cheese frosting in the glass displays made my stomach rumble. I'd hardly eaten yesterday, thanks to what happened.

"Speaking of *love*, I saw you coming out of Grain and Glass the other day."

"It isn't like that." I fidgeted with my coat.

"Maybe not yet." She grinned. "But give it time."

"I don't have time to date anyone right now, especially not one of those brothers," I said. At least I didn't give her the line about fictional guys that Grace hated so much. Who needed a relationship when I could have a bookshop? Books were much less likely to disappoint you.

"Well, aside from your refusal to admit the obvious, I'm glad you're doing okay." She bustled behind the counter, then handed me a steaming cup. "Honestly, the whole thing is ridiculous. I can't believe Leo would try to pin it on you."

Leo must be the sheriff. Nancy called everyone in town by their first name, as if she'd seen everyone and their mother grow up in Whisper Hollow.

"It means a lot that you believe it wasn't me."

"No granddaughter of Bettye's could do something like that." She ignored my card when I held it out. "This one's on the house," she said with a shake of her head.

"Thank you." I sighed, trying not to think about how they'd all been *on the house* lately.

"You know, I shouldn't be saying this to one of my best customers, but you need to get some groceries." Nancy fussed over me much like I imagined Nana would have—probably because she had no one else to fuss over with her husband dead and her kids moved out of town. "I hate to imagine you living alone and trying to run that bookshop by yourself while dealing with everything."

"I'll work on it." I stifled a sigh.

"Let me know if there's anything else I can do for you."

I took a moment to blink back the tears threatening to fall, then cleared my throat. "There are a couple of things." I pulled the scrap of paper I'd found inside *Inkheart* from my purse and held it out to her. "I found this in Nana's shop yesterday."

Nancy squinted at the design on the paper. "I've seen something similar to this at Serenity Park. Maybe you could look there. It's a block west of the town square. You can't miss it."

"Perfect." My heart jumped at the lead, and I tucked the paper away again. "I was also curious if you noticed anything strange at the festival?"

"Nothing in particular, but I wasn't there the whole time." She pursed her lips.

"I was also hoping you could tell me more about that man." I thought back on the old man in her bakery harmlessly sipping his drink even though Nancy said he'd chased Mr. James off.

"Which man?" She erased the words on the small blackboard and wrote spiced pumpkin muffins in an elegant script. "Oh, you mean Sebastian? Or Cooper? They're wonderful. You'll really—"

"No, not them," I said. "I meant Peter."

Nancy straightened and gave me a long stare. "You're not trying to say that Peter had anything to do with what happened to Marty, are you? He's far too old to have done something like that. Is this because of what I told you? Me and my silly mouth."

I shrugged and gripped the cup tighter, letting the faint heat bleeding through the plastic warm my fingers. "I don't know, but I need to find a way to clear my name, and starting with the person who has a known dislike of Mr. James seems like as good a place as any. If the police find one more piece of evidence connected to my shop, they'll probably try to arrest me then and there."

"Oh, honey." Nancy came around the counter and enveloped me in a hug. I breathed in the scent of fresh baked goods she wore like perfume. "I'll tell you what I know, but I'm not sure if it'll help."

I sniffed and pulled back. "Thank you."

She patted my hand and looked around at her empty store. "If you want to find Peter, your best bet is to go to the Blossom Boutique. He spends a lot of his afternoons there. Ask for Mr. Humphrey."

"He works at the flower shop?" Not what I expected from a potential killer, but then again, I wasn't sure what I did expect. It's not like he'd be walking around with a hammer in his belt and blood on his hands.

"He owns it. Remember, Peter owns about as much of the town as Marty does . . . did." She frowned and rubbed at an imaginary spot on the counter with her apron.

"Thank you, Nancy. I appreciate it."

"Be careful, dear. I can't imagine Peter doing something awful like this, but someone did, and I hate to think of you stirring up trouble." She pushed a tendril of hair behind her ear that had fallen out of her loose bun.

I gave her what I hoped was a reassuring smile. "I'll be careful."

Nancy opened her mouth, then closed it.

"What's wrong?"

"It's a little too convenient that you're the first person to move to town in years—ever since the Moore brothers came—and now a dead body shows up in your shop." She twisted her apron strings around her fingers while a sense of foreboding settled over me. "I'm worried about you."

My head spun from what she was implying. I didn't know anyone in town enough for them to want to frame me for murder. Unless not knowing anyone was exactly the problem. I was the perfect scapegoat.

"Just be careful," Nancy said with another troubled look.

"I will." I walked outside, taking a sip of my caramel apple cider. The burst of sugar in the sweet, buttery flavor was what I needed to knock me out of my shock and help me think. Why would someone choose me to take the fall? I hadn't been in Whisper Hollow long enough to offend anyone. Could I have been chosen because the killer knew I was new? Maybe they even knew I lived alone and wouldn't have an alibi.

I shivered at the thought, then shoved it away. No one wanted to do me harm. I was being silly. Besides, I was walking down Main Street in the middle of the morning. I'd be fine.

Though, I was going to confront a potential killer . . . so there was that.

I crossed the street to walk in the sunlight instead of the shade. Most people bustled past me without a second glance, a benefit of being new, but a few stared me down for a little too long. Either they'd already heard the rumors or they were trying to place the unfamiliar face.

Instead of making eye contact with them, I admired the decorations on Main Street. Halloween was one of my favorite holidays, along with Christmas, but with a murder hanging over my head, the season had never felt quite so scary before.

The wind whistled down the street, rustling the dry leaves under-foot and making the branches overhead sway. A few red and orange leaves drifted to the ground as they stopped clinging to life. The shop to my left, Main Street Mercantile, had pumpkins, scarecrows, and cornstalks standing guard by the front door. Large spiderwebs, hanging bats, and jack-o'-lanterns filled the display window of the next shop, Rustic Treasures, which appeared to be some sort of antique store.

The next shop bore the name Blossom Boutique painted on a wooden sign that hung above the door.

Found it.

A large wreath of dried corn husks, twigs, and adorably tiny scarecrows hung around the sign. The floral arrangements in the display window fit the fall feel as well. Orange roses, yellow carnations, and burgundy chrysanthemums sat arranged in ceramic pumpkin vases. Some displays even had miniature broomsticks, tiny witches' hats, and fake spiderweb accents to weave a bit of Halloween magic into them.

I hesitated, resting one hand on the cool metal doorknob. If I didn't go in, I wouldn't get any answers, and I couldn't sit around and wait for the police to come with more questions.

Pushing aside my reservations, I stepped inside. The motion set off a wind chime above the door, filling the floral-scented air with a gentle metallic ringing. It sure didn't feel like the store of a killer. Then again, neither did my store, and that didn't make me any less of a suspect.

"Welcome to Blossom Boutique. How can I help you?" A cheerful woman smiled at me from where she stood at a wooden table in the center of the shop showcasing an assortment of decorative potted plants. She looked to be somewhere in her fifties.

"I'm looking for Mr. Humphrey. Is he around?"

"I'm sorry. He left last night."

My pulse picked up speed. "Did he say where he was going?"

"Family business." She dusted one of the ceramic pots.

"Do you know what time he left here two nights ago?" I asked as casually as I could while hoping she fell into the gossipy half of the town.

"I'm not sure." She pursed her lips. "It was past eight when I went home, and he was still here. So sometime after that."

If he'd been at the shop on his own from eight p.m. on, he would've had plenty of time to kill Mr. James during that three-hour window.

"I see." I hesitated a moment, unsure of what else to do. "Well, thank you for your help."

"My pleasure, honey," she said. "Would you like to leave a message for him or anything?"

"Oh, that's okay. I'll try again later. Do you know when he'll be back?"

"In a few days, I believe. He wasn't sure yet."

"Thank you." I pulled open the door and escaped back into the bright sunlight.

When my phone buzzed with a text in my pocket, I pulled it out, then did a double take at the name on the screen. My stomach dropped to my toes, and I sucked in a breath.

What on earth did Tate want?

Chapter 6

Serenity Park

I glared down at the screen, my hand shaking from how hard I gripped the phone. What was the egotistical jerk up to now? I opened the text and skimmed Tate's message.

I miss you, Harp. Can we talk? Call me.

Ha. Like I would. That idiot had had his last chance. I stuffed an AirPod into one ear and called Grace, who picked up after a few rings.

"I don't think you called me this much when you lived here."

"That's because I was over every day." I made my way back down Main Street.

"True." Her teasing tone shifted into one that was more serious. "Any updates with the case?"

"Not really. I tried to talk to the man Nancy mentioned, but he left town last night."

The sound of clinking dishes came from her end, followed by rushing water. "Suspicious, but I guess you won't know more until he gets back."

"Yeah, but I realized something last night," I said. "As the owner, wouldn't Mr. James have had his own key to Whispering Pages?"

"It's a possibility."

"And if so, he could've let himself into the store, which opens up the pool of suspects to anyone walking by, which could've been a lot of people since it was the night of the town festival."

"Make sure to mention it to the sheriff."

"I will," I said. "Though, I have no idea why he'd come by so late. Maybe he was at the festival and decided that while he was in a good mood, he'd swing by and drop off that note about wanting to kick me out."

"The jerk." Almost as an afterthought, Grace added, "Bless his soul."

"Yup." I chewed on my bottom lip for a moment while deciding whether I should tell her about Tate or not.

"So what else happened?"

"What do you mean?"

"Something else happened," she said, as if she could see it written on my face from my tone.

Why had I even tried? There was no keeping secrets from Grace—none that lasted anyway. "Tate texted me."

"What?" She let out a string of expletives, then a kid said something in the background. "I know. I'm sorry. I'll put money in the swear jar later, sweetie."

I could faintly make out the sound of one of her sons singing a tuneless song that sounded like, "Mommy's paying for our next family vacay!" I bit back a smile.

"What did he say?" Grace asked a minute later, once things were quieter on her end.

I lowered my voice as I approached Grain and Glass. It would be my luck to have Sebastian or Cooper overhear me talking about my terrible ex. "He said he misses me and wants to talk."

"He's out of his mind."

"I know."

"You need to delete that loser's number."

"I know." I ducked my head at a couple walking down the street but kept walking without making eye contact. I wasn't extroverted at the best of times, and being suspected in a murder case wasn't the best of times for me.

"And block him."

"I know . . ."

"Harp?"

"Grace?"

"That didn't sound like a commitment."

I sighed. "I *should* block him, but it's kind of nice knowing what he's thinking. This way he can't spring something on me."

Grace scoffed. "Like he's going to drive all the way to Whisper Hollow and surprise you or something?"

"Yeah . . . no . . . I dunno." I ran a hand through my too-short hair again. He used to enjoy surprising me when we were dating, but I guess that didn't matter anymore.

"So let me get this straight. You hate him enough to pick up your life and move to a brand-new place while listening to *Before He Cheats* for hours in the car, but you don't hate him enough to block his number?"

"When you put it that way, it sounds pathetic."

"Hate to break it to you, Harp, but it is pathetic."

I pulled my coat tighter against the stiff wind. "You always know the right thing to say."

"Look, all I'm saying is, nothing good will come out of holding on to that loser."

"I know, I know. Can we talk about something else?" I made it back to Whispering Pages and found Jiji sitting outside the door. How she'd even made it back to town was beyond me since she'd been MIA earlier that morning. But her presence almost felt like a sign that I should open the shop up instead of going home and doing nothing all afternoon. After all, Mr. James's death didn't get me out of paying rent. If I didn't owe him, I'd probably owe the bank.

"Yeah, sure. What are you doing now? Heading home?"

"I think I'm going to open the shop for the afternoon."

"A murder just happened there."

"Gee, thanks, Grace." I rolled my eyes and unlocked the front door. "And the police didn't say I couldn't. If I go home now, I'll miss out on a day of potential sales, and I already missed yesterday since the shop had to stay closed so I could get it cleaned. I need the money now more than ever, especially after having to pay for the cleaning."

"Fair enough, but do you think people will come after what happened?"

"I don't know, but at least this way I can stay busy."

"If things get too tight, you can always try to get a loan from the bank. Don't let it stress you out too much."

My stomach tightened. "Mmhmm. Good idea. For now, though, I'll give Kyle a few days off. It'll save money and not be so awkward." Luckily, I could afford to pay him a little while longer. He was leaving in a month or two anyway.

But doing that, I realized too late, left me alone in the shop. And no matter how hard I tried, I couldn't stop my gaze from drifting to the spot on the floor where I'd found Mr. James's body. Could Kyle have taken the money? No, it wouldn't make sense. He wouldn't have even known where to look, and my office was locked most of the time.

I stayed on the phone with Grace while I ate lunch and tidied up the store until the front door jingled.

"I have a customer. Tell Jeff and the kids hi. I gotta go," I whispered before hanging up.

But when I turned around, it wasn't a customer standing by the front door. It was Kyle.

"What are you doing here?" I folded my arms across my chest.

"I wanted to apologize for what I told the police," he mumbled, scuffing his foot against the floor.

"Really?"

"My mom is a friend of Mrs. Simmon, and she said there was no way you'd do something like that." He looked pretty much anywhere but at me. "Plus, I need this job."

Ah, there it was. The real reason he'd come. But I shouldn't complain. With Kyle at work, I was free to get sales *and* pursue the lead at the park.

"I appreciate your apology"—as halfhearted as it was—"and I'd love it if you could work this afternoon."

He looked up. "You serious?"

"Definitely," I said, already moving toward the door. "I have a few things I need to look into, so it would be great if you kept an eye on the store."

"I'll take care of everything."

I walked back outside and retraced my steps down Main Street toward the town square, then I headed west. Like Nancy had said, an ornate wrought iron gate with the words Serenity Park came into view. I stepped under the vines and ivy intertwined around its arches. Tall oak and maple trees, whose leaves were ablaze with fall colors, formed a canopy overhead. A small tranquil pond reflected the azure sky and the few clouds drifting across its surface. In the distance stood a gazebo adorned with pumpkins and cornstalks.

No wonder it was called Serenity Park. It was beautiful, with nothing suspicious in sight. But I was led to the park for a reason, and I needed to find out why. I turned my footsteps toward a woman sitting on a weathered wooden bench lining the gravel walkway.

Something about her reminded me of Grace. Maybe it was the horde of kids. Or the way her honey-colored hair cascaded down her back in loose waves and shimmered with auburn highlights as it caught the sun. Or her exercise clothes that reminded me of Grace trying to get her daily yoga in while her kids swarmed her. Maybe I could ask her a few questions.

"Beautiful day, isn't it?" I said as I got close.

"Sure is." She smiled at me, then shifted her attention to the gaggle of children playing on the playground.

"I'm Harper, by the way." I held out a hand to her.

"I'm Jessie." She shook it. "And that's Jake, Lila, Lukas, and Izzy."

I laughed. "I'm not going to remember all of those."

"That's okay, there won't be a quiz later." She patted for me to join her on the bench. "You new in town?"

"Yes. I took over my grandmother's bookshop, Whispering Pages." I leaned against the back of the sun-warmed bench.

Her eyes widened. "Oh. I didn't realize you were Bettye's granddaughter."

"You knew her?"

"This is Whisper Hollow. Everyone knows everyone." She laughed. "And I used to take the kids into the shop all the time. They loved it. We were all heartbroken when Bettye passed."

"Thank you." I wasn't sure if that was the correct response, but I also wasn't sure what else to say.

"Once things settle down, we'll have to swing by again to visit," she said. "The kids would love that."

Something told me Jessie and I could be friends—though my track record proved that I was about as bad at picking friends as boyfriends. "So would I."

"Well, I'd better gather the kids." She stood and stretched. "It's getting close to nap time, and if I don't make it, they're monsters the rest of the day while we wait for their mother to get home."

My eyes widened. I'd thought the kids were hers, but she must've been a sitter.

"Before you leave, can I ask you a question?" I stood and fished the scrap of paper from my purse. "Have you seen this design anywhere around here?"

Jessie smiled and pointed in the distance. "Of course. It's over there by the gazebo. You'll find it on the sign that talks about the park."

"Thank you." I waved goodbye to her and headed to the gazebo while she rounded up the kids. With the sun on my face, the playful breeze wasn't as cold as it had been, and I enjoyed the short walk, despite the looming mystery of Nana's missing money and Mr. James's killer. Who might have done it, and how were the two events related?

I stopped and debated turning around. The gazebo wasn't empty.

Sebastian snapped a notebook shut and glanced up at me, looking unfairly attractive in his blue jeans and sweater. Maybe it was that he wasn't covered in sawdust or that his eyes weren't red and watering from being pepper sprayed. But it didn't change how he set me on edge. In fact, it made it worse. Attractive guys were not to be trusted.

"Sorry," I said stiffly. "I didn't realize you were here. I'll leave."

"You don't have to. It's a public park."

Not an invitation, but it would do since I still needed to look at the sign.

"Thanks." I averted my gaze and wandered to the small white plaque that talked about the park. Holding the paper up, I realized the mysterious design was part of a flower. The same shape was etched around the sign's border.

"That's our state flower," Sebastian said from next to me.

I jumped. I hadn't heard him approach. Or realized how tall he was. "Really?" My voice came out weirdly breathless. I cleared my throat. "I didn't know that."

He held his notebook to his side—what was he hiding?—and nodded. "Yup, they're all over the park." He gestured around, and I recognized the small pink flower next to the gazebo and the faint pink color in the distance by the pond as well.

"Interesting," I murmured, my mind racing. Finding flowers at the park wasn't unusual, but it had to mean something that it'd been part of a flower I'd found in place of Nana's missing money and that Mr. Humphrey, my number one murder suspect, worked at Whisper Hollow's flower shop. The two were connected, and I needed to figure out how.

"Well, I better get back to work," Sebastian said.

"Oh, okay. Bye." I saw what Cooper meant when he said Sebastian didn't like people. Or maybe it was just me. Or maybe he didn't want me to know what he was doing at the gazebo. Clearly, he had a secret. Then again, I supposed we all did. I thought about what I hadn't told Grace about Tate and bit my lip.

As Sebastian walked away, a duck from the pond honked at him and flapped its wings. I smiled. At least he didn't have every animal wrapped around his finger like he did Jiji. Somehow, the duck not liking him gave me leeway not to get along with him either.

Unsure of what else to do, I searched the gazebo and the surrounding area. A small sign near a bunch of flowers said they had been donated by Lillian. Maybe that was my next clue. If she had something to do with the flowers, it was at least worth looking into. I scribbled down her name so I wouldn't forget and hurried back to the shop.

"Cooper Moore came by while you were gone," Kyle said almost as soon as I entered.

"Oh? What did he want?" Should I ask Nancy if she knew a Lillian? How would I find her?

"I'm not sure, but he left you a message by the register." Kyle pointed to a piece of paper on the desk, then returned to shelving a few books.

"Thanks. You can go after you finish stocking that shelf. I'll handle the last few hours on my own." I picked up the note and examined the bold, masculine writing.

Harperella,

You're one hard woman to catch, and you didn't even leave behind your shoe to help me find you. I wanted to run this new nickname by you, but even as I wrote it, I think I've realized I'll keep trying.

Until next time.

-Coop

P.S. This means we're friends, and you can call me Coop.

I smile at the note. Maybe being friends with Cooper wouldn't be the worst thing, as long as I didn't give him a way to hurt me. It would make Grace happy, knowing I was making friends my age in town, but, then again, if she knew I was friends with a man, she'd have all sorts of expectations.

Wait, what was I doing? I didn't have time to be distracted by a funny man. I needed to focus on my immediate problems. All that mattered was saving the shop and my reputation.

I pulled a pen and scrap of paper from my purse and scribbled a note about finding out who Lillian was so I wouldn't forget. She was my next clue to finding out what happened to Nana's money.

Chapter 7

Kneading the Perfect Alibi

Despite Grace's skepticism, the next few days passed with a steady stream of customers coming in and out of Whispering Pages, though only a fraction of them translated to actual sales. Curiosity killed the cat, and it also drove them to gawk at the person suspected of killing Mr. James, like I was some sort of circus attraction.

With Mr. Humphrey still out of town and Nancy having no idea who Lillian was, there wasn't much for me to do besides focus on the bookshop, but the impending rent payment did little to get my mind off the murder or the missing money.

I saw Mr. James's body every time I looked at the skeleton in the display case. I remembered finding the hammer every time I walked by the sci-fi shelf. I even heard the squish of blood under my shoes. But I pushed it all away because I wouldn't let this be the end of me or Nana's shop. Mr. James hadn't believed I could run Whispering Pages, and Sheriff Warner hadn't believed I could be innocent, but I'd prove both of them wrong. If there was anything I hated more than cheating, lying exes, it was people telling me what I couldn't do.

Nancy came in as my last customer left. Well, not *customer*, since the teenager in a baggy sweater had only browsed the store's small collection of manga before leaving with a disappointed sigh. But positive thinking was better than the alternative.

"How are things going, dear?" She leaned against the counter, leaving a smudge of flour on the polished wood.

I wiped at it and sighed. "Fine."

"You know, in Asia, they say every time you sigh, you let a little bit of your happiness slip away."

"Did you learn that in your K-dramas too?"

"Possibly," she said with a small smile.

"I guess I'm a little down because even though I've had a steady stream of customers, few have bought anything."

Nancy tsked and shook her head. "Another slew of customers coming in because of the gossip, eh? Shame on them, but you know what they say. Bad publicity is still publicity."

I held back a smile. If gossip was an Olympic sport, Nancy would have a gold medal.

"I should be grateful they're coming in at all. I wasn't sure anyone would want to come because of . . . well, you know."

"Because it's *haunted*." She made air quotes. "Maybe you can focus on that for your sales."

"That's a good idea. I already have some spooky stories and murder mysteries out for Halloween, but I can put out more if you think it's a good idea." I moved out from behind the counter and linked my arm through hers. "For now, I need one of your sandwiches for dinner, then I'm going to head home and watch the extended version of *The Fellowship of the Ring*."

"I've got a better idea than a movie by yourself." She led me outside into the chilled evening air.

I locked up the shop and followed her to Sugarplum Delights—somehow, I still hadn't gotten around to doing any serious grocery shopping. Cooking wasn't my forte, and with Nancy next door, it was hard to find the motivation to try.

"So what's the big surprise?" I asked as we walked into her mostly empty shop. The scent of cinnamon, nutmeg, and cloves permeated the air. Nancy's bakery always smelled delicious.

Two dark heads swiveled to face us from the single occupied table.

I yanked on her arm. "Nancy, please tell me this isn't a setup."

"I can't," she whispered back. "But at least it isn't the kind that will land you in jail." At my grimace, she added, "Sorry, too soon?"

"A bit." I sighed again as she led me toward the table where Sebastian and Cooper sat next to each other.

"Enjoy yourself for a while," she said in a not-quiet-at-all voice before heading to the counter.

Cooper gave me a wide smile, then stood and pulled out a chair across from him. "I didn't know you'd be joining us tonight, Harper-oo."

"Me either," I muttered as I dropped into the proffered chair and angled myself so the vase of sunflowers and dried wheat stalks blocked most of my view of Sebastian's face. If he was disappointed I was there, I didn't want to see it.

"How was your day?" Cooper's fingers drummed across the table.

"I've had better and worse. How about you two?"

A corner of Cooper's mouth rose as if he knew I was trying to deflect the conversation. It made his smile lopsided and adorable. "It couldn't have been that bad. Seemed like you had a steady stream of customers today."

"Were you paying attention?" I asked with a laugh. Attractive, friendly guys were *not* to be trusted. Hadn't I learned my lesson from Tate?

"Are you surprised?" He winked at me, somehow making it look flirty and not creepy, which most people never managed. "I like to keep an eye on all the attractive women in town." As Nancy bustled back over with my sandwich, he added, "That's why I spend so much time over here."

"Cooper Moore, that smooth tongue of yours is going to get you in trouble one day," she said with a wide smile.

"It already has," Sebastian muttered from across the table. At the mention of trouble, I remembered running into Sebastian at the park and how he'd tried to hide something from me.

"And that surly attitude of yours will do the same for you, Sebastian," Nancy said. While I tried to suppress a smirk, she gave him a hard stare and added, "If you smiled once in a while, you'd be fighting the ladies off just like your brother."

Sebastian grimaced as if the thought was horrifying, though the tips of his ears were pink. He cut his gaze to me, and I shifted to put the plants between us again.

"So why don't you look happy?" Cooper asked again.

"It's not a big deal." I took a bite of my sandwich, and the flavors burst to life on my tongue. The crunch of the toasted bread. The spicy sweetness of the jalapeño-blackberry jam, and the combination of Swiss cheese and bacon. How would I find the motivation to cook for myself with Nancy's delicious meals so close?

After another bite, where Cooper still watched me, I said, "I'm worried about the shop."

"We get that, right Seb?" Cooper nodded at his brother. "Paying rent is one of those things that's always weighing on the back of your mind."

"Right?" I said.

Cooper rested one of his large, warm hands over mine. I glanced at Sebastian, then pulled my hand free to take another bite. Did Cooper always flirt so forwardly?

He reminded me too much of Tate—one strike against him.

Once I swallowed, I said, "Dealing with the murder and the shop at the same time is a lot."

"Are the police still treating you like a suspect?" Sebastian's sudden contribution to the conversation threw me off guard, and I answered a smidge too honestly.

"Yes, which is why I'm trying to find the killer to prove my innocence."

"You shouldn't do that," Sebastian said. "It could be dangerous."

"Or exciting," Cooper said. "Any leads?"

"Not really, and I don't have another option. The shop will go under for sure if I end up arrested." I took a long sip of my ice water, wishing it would cool the heat rising in my cheeks. Talking about my failing business and semi-criminal background with two attractive men wasn't my idea of a good time.

"Why don't you give them an alibi?" Sebastian's matter-of-fact tone made it clear he thought I was an idiot for not having done so sooner.

I gritted my teeth but tried to keep my expression neutral. "I'd love to, but I don't have an alibi. I was home alone that night."

"Don't worry about him. He's a grump with everyone. He doesn't know that grumpy geeks are out." Cooper patted my hand again. "Though, it's a shame you missed the festival. We could've danced when I wasn't working the booth."

"I'm not great at dancing." I peeked around the centerpiece, trying to imagine the buff, sexy Sebastian that way. "You're a nerd?"

He scowled. "Is there something wrong with that?"

"Um, no." Just that I was as susceptible to nerds as humans were to the One Ring.

"But as entertaining as it is to make fun of Seb"—Cooper kept talking over his brother's grunt of protest—"let's focus on you. Is there anything we can do to help?"

"Thanks," I said, "but I don't think so."

"If you want, I can tell the sheriff you were with me that night," Cooper said with a seductive wink.

I flushed. "Um, that seems—"

Sebastian hit him over the back of the head. "Stop joking around, Coop. You can't lie about these things."

Cooper laughed. "I was kidding, but I will talk to the sheriff and see if I can put in a good word for you."

"Thank you." I wasn't sure how much a *good word* would accomplish, but at this point, I'd take all the help I could get.

The door opened, and a woman walked into the bakery—the woman I'd spoken to at Blossom Boutique.

"Hi, Lillian," Cooper said while Sebastian waved.

"Sorry, I can't stop to chat. I'm in a hurry." The woman waved back but went straight to the counter.

I straightened in my seat and leaned closer to Sebastian. "That's Lillian?" Considering she worked at the flower shop, it wouldn't have been strange for her to donate flowers to the park.

Lillian chatted with Nancy while waiting for her food. Based on their body language, the two seemed to be acquaintances at least. So why had Nancy said she didn't know anyone named Lillian?

Cooper looked at me. "And why are you so curious about Lillian?"

"I didn't realize that was her," I said, thinking fast. "I met her at the flower shop and didn't know it was the same person." Even though Cooper had asked if I'd made any progress on the case, it felt too early to tell him my fledgling suspicions.

"That's no surprise," Cooper said. "If I remember correctly, she's Mr. Humphrey's daughter."

"She is?" My eyes widened, and I looked at Lillian once more. She certainly hadn't mentioned *that* when I'd talked to her, which seemed strange. There were plenty of opportunities to slip it into our earlier conversation.

A few minutes later, Nancy handed over a bag of food, and Lillian strolled from the store.

"Excuse me." I rose from the table. "I need to talk to Nancy." I wanted to talk to Lillian too, but now that I knew where she worked, I could talk to her any time. First, I had to find out why Nancy had lied.

"How was your dinner, Harper?" Nancy asked with a wide grin.

I rolled my eyes. "Delicious, of course."

"That's not—"

"I thought you said you didn't know Lillian," I said before her questions turned into the Spanish Inquisition.

Her eyes widened. "I don't."

"But Cooper and Sebastian said that was Lillian you were talking to a moment ago."

"Oh." She hit her forehead with her palm. "Silly me. I forgot. When she was a kid she went by Kylie, her middle name, but when she moved back to town she decided to go by Lillian again."

"Oh, I guess that makes sense," I said. "I met her at the flower shop."

"That's not strange. She works with Peter a few days a week." Nancy tidied up the area around the register.

"Yes, but she didn't mention he was her father." I leaned against the counter and lowered my voice. "Don't you think that's strange?"

Nancy blinked. "Not particularly."

I bit my lip. I hadn't told Nancy about the missing money or what that flower design meant, so she didn't know about the suspicious connection between the two, but I knew what I had to do next: talk to Lillian.

Chapter 8

The Silmarillion

"I've got three weeks to scrounge up a thousand more dollars for the rent before the end of the month, and if the days continue as they have, I won't make it," I said to Grace a few mornings later on the phone as I glanced over Nana's accounting books. "I don't know if I can do it." Why had I thought I could?

"Yes, you can, Harp. You're one of the most determined people I know."

"But even when I get people into the shop, it doesn't mean they'll buy anything." I closed the book with a sigh. To give myself something to do besides biting my nails, I grabbed a bag of candy to refill the cauldron near the display window. "And besides, yesterday and today there's been hardly anyone coming in." Now that the gossip had died down, so had the shop's traffic.

"Let's be serious. I'm doing a terrible job at saving Whispering Pages." I couldn't stand the idea of losing Nana's shop after I'd already lost her, but the bookshop might end up on my growing list of failures.

Grace made a thoughtful noise. "It isn't over yet. What you need is a way to get people in again, but then you also need a way to make them buy some books. Maybe a sale or something?"

"So your suggestion to me not having enough money is to sell my books for even cheaper?"

"At least then you'd be getting *some* sales. If you don't want to do that, you could also try doing something like a local author spotlight. Or like a book subscription service. Ooh, I know. You could host a monthly book club."

"I don't know if that'll work while I'm still a suspect in a murder investigation."

"Well, you're going back to talk to that Peter guy today, aren't you?"

"Yeah, if he's back. Hopefully, I'll figure something out." I spent the next minutes filling Grace in on how Blossom Boutique had been closed every time I'd checked, and I hadn't been able to find Mr. Humphrey or his daughter, Lillian. So much for being able to talk to her whenever.

Around noon, the door jingled, and a woman about my age walked in wearing a colorful Maxi dress. Her gaze darted to me, then away. "Sorry to bother you."

"Oh, not at all," I said. "What can I help you with?"

"Sounds like you've got a customer. I'll let you go," Grace said before the line went dead with a click.

"Actually, I'm looking for a book," the woman said. Her black hair was pulled back in a thick bun, and her darker skin matched her deep-brown eyes.

"Then you're in the right place," I said with a smile. "Which one would you like?"

She walked in and tripped over a display of jack-o'-lanterns mixed with white gourds near the front.

"Are you okay?"

"I'm fine. I'm so sorry," she said as she tried to gather the spilled pumpkins and straighten the display.

"Don't worry about it." I knelt and helped reorganize the display, then gave her a hand up. "Now what can I help you find?"

She gave an embarrassed shrug. "It's a bit nerdy—"

"Then you fit in well here." I flashed her a customer service smile that didn't feel at all forced.

"I'm looking for *The Silmarillion*."

"*The Silmarillion*?" My thoughts returned to the book in the bag I'd found on my porch, which I'd brought back to Whispering Pages.

"Yes, my mother bought it for me a few days ago, but then lost the book before she could give it to me. So I told her I'd swing by and grab another."

I walked to the front table and found Jiji sitting on the counter, purring contentedly. "As strange as this is, I think I found the book you're talking about. Do you have the receipt by chance?" More like it found me, considering it had shown up on my front porch.

"Really?" She looked at me excitedly, meeting my gaze for the first time since coming in. "That would be wonderful, and I don't think so. Mom said she put it in the book . . . which she lost, obviously."

"That sounds like the one I found. I could've sworn I put it somewhere over here." I lifted a few things off the counter, checking under piles of papers.

"I'm María, by the way."

"Harper."

After another minute of me searching fruitlessly, María looked around with a wistful sigh. "I just love bookstores and libraries."

"A room with no books is like a body with no soul," I said as I kept searching the desk.

"Patrick Rothfuss?" she asked with a smile.

"It's nice to meet a fellow geek. Most wouldn't have realized I was quoting *The Name of the Wind*."

She reached out and let Jiji sniff her hand. "Cute cat."

"Sometimes." When she isn't running into a stranger's shop or finding murder weapons.

María moved to pet Jiji, but the cat hopped off the counter, revealing the book in question.

"You found it!"

"Yeah, sorry about Jiji sitting on it." I pulled the book out of the bag and checked for damages while brushing off some cat fur. Though Jiji had squashed the bag, the book was in good condition.

She laughed. "That's okay. I like a cat with good taste."

Too bad she didn't have better taste in men. I thought back on how Sebastian had practically thrown her out of the shop. Granted, she had messed up a project he was working on, but still. Who didn't like cats?

María hesitated by the desk, holding the book against her chest. "You know, I don't think it's true what they say."

"What who say?"

"People in town."

Nice and specific. I tidied up the counter to give my hands something to do.

"I don't think you're guilty."

"That's good to hear." I wasn't sure what the correct response to that was. *Thank you? Me too?* "Not that I want people to suspect me, but since half the town already does, why don't you?"

"I just find it hard to believe. Anyone who quotes Patrick Rothfuss doesn't seem like the murdering type."

Was there a murdering type? "Thank you."

"Well"—María looked around the shop, then back to me—"I guess I should get going."

"Feel free to come back. We've got a great fantasy section I'm sure you'll enjoy if you're a Tolkien fan."

She glanced toward the corner where the word *Fantasy* hung on a sign draped in cobwebs. "Maybe I'll check it out before I go. I've still got some time."

"Great!" I wouldn't complain about another potential sale, and maybe even a potential friend. As long as I could convince myself to trust her. But in a town where I was looking at everyone as a potential suspect, trusting people was proving harder than it used to.

María and I chatted for the next few minutes about our favorite books and hobbies while I recommended a few different reads to her. She was surprisingly easy to talk to, despite her earlier shyness. Or maybe that was just nerves about walking into a potential murderer's shop. Even if she didn't think I was guilty, it was probably still nerve-wracking.

The bell jingled, reminding me I should get back to work. "Feel free to keep browsing." I turned to the front door with a smile, then froze.

Sheriff Warner stood at the entrance.

I'd been dreading his visit all week. I hadn't been able to make as much progress with the case as I'd hoped and had done little to clear my name. Now he'd come to arrest me.

"Harper Coleman."

I swallowed and tried to ignore my pounding heart. "Yes?"

"We need to talk."

"O-of course." I swallowed hard and gestured to the winding staircase against the back wall that would take us to where Kyle had been questioned after we'd discovered the body. "We can go to the second floor."

Sheriff Warner's gaze flicked to María, who met his gaze, then ducked behind a bookshelf. "That would be good," he said.

My heartbeat grew louder and matched the thud of my footsteps as we walked up the spiral staircase. One stair creaked ominously, and I couldn't help but glance over my shoulder at the sheriff. Had he come to arrest me?

The thud of my shoes on the hardwood floor upstairs matched my pounding heart and a weight sat on my chest. Antique mirrors dripping with fake cobwebs continued the Halloween feel on the second floor. I claimed a chair, and the sheriff took another in the children's corner. They were far too comfy and casual, considering the tension flowing through me.

"I'm guessing this is about Mr. James," I said to break the building silence. I wasn't a fan of long silences when I was a nervous wreck. I fidgeted with the crystal ball that sat on the table between us.

He nodded, and his hat tipped down. "It is. Some new information has come to light. And I'm afraid—"

My pulse thundered in my ears, trying to drown out his words. I stared down at my hands, which were clenched in my lap.

"I owe you an apology."

"I'm telling you it wasn't me." I blinked. "Wait, what?"

He cleared his throat. "You're clear of any suspicions or charges. I'm sorry you were dragged into this."

"I don't understand." Relief and confusion swirled in my stomach, making me lightheaded.

"It means we don't think you're guilty anymore."

"Thank goodness. I thought you'd come to haul me away." I exhaled loudly, and my shoulders slumped forward. "What changed?"

"Your alibi checked out for the time of the murder," he said. "Also, while the blood on the hammer was a match for Mr. James, the fingerprints weren't yours."

"My alibi?" My confusion allowed the words to spew forth even as relief tentatively settled in.

He rubbed his borderline double chin. "Yes, one of the Moore brothers said they went by your house that night and saw you at home around eleven, passed out on your couch. And that's right in the middle of our murder window, so we've ruled you out as a suspect."

I blinked. Had Cooper lied to the police so I'd have an alibi?

"He said he had to drop something off," he added almost as an afterthought.

His words helped everything click into place like a missing puzzle piece. The book I'd discovered on my porch. Cooper must've dropped it off, and that's how it ended up there. I wasn't sure why he hadn't returned to the store or said anything at dinner last night, but whatever his reasoning, he'd saved me. I couldn't help the smile that spread across my face. I was free and, hopefully, that would help the shop too. But I couldn't celebrate yet. The murderer was still out there, and they'd still tried to frame me. Plus, Nana's money was missing, and I had the rent to worry about.

"Anyway, we've ruled you out, but since the body was discovered in your shop, you might still have officers coming by now and then until we get the case wrapped up."

"I understand." At least, I understood that, though my name had been cleared, my business might still be in danger until the actual suspect was caught. If the suspect wasn't caught, the open case would continue to be associated with Whispering Pages. And if I wanted to help my shop and find Nana's missing money, I still needed to find the killer. "Thank you for letting me know."

I followed him down the stairs and to the front door. He tipped his hat to me with a final "we'll be in touch" and let the door click shut behind him.

"See, I knew you were innocent!" María emerged from between two of the shelves and gave me a wide smile.

I returned the smile and made a mental note to have my next meeting in my office. Despite the Halloween music playing in the background, sound still traveled throughout the shop too easily. "I'm glad the police have realized it too."

"This deserves a celebration. Let's go to Sugarplum Delights and get a treat."

I laughed at her enthusiasm. "I can't yet. I'm working."

"Then how about tonight? We could meet there for dinner." She seemed almost hopeful, her brown eyes sparkling.

Though I hadn't had much luck with female friends in the past, maybe my luck would change in Whisper Hollow, especially now that I wasn't suspected of murder. "Sure, that sounds great. I can close the shop around seven. Does that sound okay?"

"Sounds perfect." She stepped back and grabbed something from a shelf, then turned to face me again, holding a stack of books. "And in the meantime, I have a few books to buy."

I laughed again and checked her out. "I need more customers like you to come around."

"You've only been open a few weeks. Give it time."

Time was the one thing I didn't have. "Right," I said with a tight smile. "Well, I'll see you tonight."

"See you," she chirped as she walked out the door with her tower of books.

Once she'd left, I worked until Kyle came in for his shift, then I ran next door to thank Cooper. For all his similarities to Tate, maybe I could trust him after all.

Inside, an elderly man wearing a pair of suspenders and a bowling cap stood near a display on the left wall, talking to Sebastian. They stood in front of a familiar rocking chair.

The door jingled, and Sebastian glanced at me. Our eyes met, and a thrill ran through me.

"So you think this will be a good fit?" the older man asked, reclaiming Sebastian's attention.

"I think she's going to love the rocking chair, Mr. Mosely." Sebastian smiled at the man, seeming more relaxed with him than he'd ever been with me. "Besides, it's a little late to change your mind. It's already paid for, and I'm almost done."

"I really need to find the perfect gift." The older man took off his hat and rubbed his bald head with a handkerchief he pulled from his pocket.

"Based on what you told me, I'm confident you made a good choice. I think she's going to love it."

I took a step forward, then rocked back on my heels. Sure, I'd barged into the back the other day to chase after Jiji, but I shouldn't go back there again. It'd be best to wait for Sebastian to finish with his customer, then ask him where I could find Cooper.

Mr. Mosely nodded once, then looked at Sebastian with his thick white eyebrows pulled together. "You might think I'm being dramatic, but it's hard to find the perfect wedding anniversary gift after fifty-two years. And the perfect woman deserves the perfect gift, don't you think?"

Sebastian clapped the older man on the shoulder. "Does the perfect woman even exist?"

"Elly is the perfect woman for me, and that's all I could ask for." Mr. Mosely looked up at him and wiggled his thick eyebrows.

"Well, I should be able to get the chair finished by the end of the day, and I'll deliver it straight to your house to make sure it's on time."

"Thank you."

"No, thank *you* for being understanding about the delay. I'm sorry it wasn't ready for you to pick up."

A sinking feeling in my gut told me why the chair hadn't been ready on time and why it looked familiar. It was the project Sebastian had been working on when Jiji broke into the shop. No wonder he'd been so terse.

"This seems like the better option, anyway." Mr. Mosely laughed. "Unloading it is probably more than my old back can handle these days. I might look like I'm in my fifties, but I'm almost eighty-five, you know. I shouldn't be hauling around rocking chairs willy-nilly."

"Of course not." Sebastian escorted the older man to the door.

I stepped out of their way, unable to meet Sebastian's gaze, but once the door closed behind Mr. Mosely, it was just the two of us left in the shop.

"Can I help you?" he asked in a polite tone.

"I'm sorry about the chair." Unable to hold it in any longer, I blurted the words out. "Jiji is the reason you couldn't finish it in time, right?"

"Jiji?" He raised one dark eyebrow, making him look like Cooper. Or maybe Cooper looked like him. "Like *Kiki's Delivery Service* Jiji?"

I blinked at him, surprised he knew the reference. "Yeah, that was one of my favorite movies as a kid, so Nana and I used to watch it all the time." I shook my head. "Anyway, I know she messed something up when she ran in here the other day."

He shrugged his broad shoulders and looked away. "Those things happen."

The door to the backroom opened, and Cooper poked his head out. "I thought I heard your voice, Harperoni. To what do we owe the pleasure?"

I forced my gaze from the older brother to the younger one. "I was hoping to talk to you," I said while trying not to pay attention to how Sebastian disappeared into the back room again. "Also, I think the nicknames are getting worse."

"I know. I'll keep trying." He shook his head in mock despair. "But great timing. I was about to take a break for lunch. Care to join me?"

"I shouldn't be gone too long."

Cooper crossed the room in a few long strides and held the door open. "Then I'll walk you back," he said with his signature bow.

I smiled and walked back into the crisp air with him, resisting the urge to glance back over my shoulder at Sebastian. A brisk wind blew down the street, rustling the leaves overhead. We walked the short distance back to Whispering Pages, and I shivered in my cable-knit sweater. "You didn't need to talk to the police for me, but I'm grateful you did."

Cooper stopped and looked at me, his dark eyes widening. "What are you talking about?"

"It's too late to play innocent now." I laughed and turned to face him. "Last night you mentioned you'd talk to the police to give me an alibi, and this morning, Sheriff Warner shows up and tells me I'm off the hook for the case."

"That wasn't me."

His words made my heart pound in a heavy rhythm. If it wasn't Cooper, who'd talk to the sheriff, that left only one other *Moore brother*.

Chapter 9

The Key to Salvation or Damnation

"Are you saying it was Sebastian who talked to the police?" Even though I was the one saying the words, I still couldn't believe them. Sebastian was the one who'd driven to my house to return the book? Well, maybe I could believe it. It seemed like Sebastian—dropping it off without saying a word to me.

"It must've been." Cooper wrinkled his brow and shifted his weight from one foot to the other. "Though, I'm not sure why he didn't tell me he was at your house that night. I didn't realize he'd left the festival."

"I don't know either." And maybe I never would. Talking to Cooper, friendly approachable Cooper, who sometimes was a little too forward, was one thing. But talking to his intimidating older brother whose work I'd almost ruined was another.

"Well, anyway, I better get back to work." I gave him a faint smile. "Those books won't sell themselves."

"Wait." Cooper grabbed my hand to stop me from leaving. "I meant to ask, how are things going with your other *project*? Is there anything I can do to help?"

I squeezed his hand, then let go. "No real leads yet, but I'm going to talk to Mr. Humphrey again today, so we'll see."

"The crotchety old man who owns the flower shop?" Cooper raised an eyebrow. "Is that why you were so curious about Lillian the other day? You think she's connected to the murder?"

"Something like that." I thought she was connected to one case and her father to another, but since I also believed the two went hand in hand, this might be my chance to get things straightened out.

"Well, good luck," he said. "Let me know if you ever want me to go with you so you aren't talking to people alone."

"Thanks, Cooper." At his mock glare, I changed it to "Coop."

He waved and walked down the street while I entered Whispering Pages. For the rest of the afternoon, my thoughts went in circles while I tidied the shop and tried to think of more ways to get customers to come in. Grace's suggestions circled around in my head. Even with the police exonerating me, I needed more to help business pick up.

After a few hours of no one coming in, I sent Kyle home, closed up the store an hour early, and headed down Main Street. The best thing I could do was clear the shop's reputation by finding the culprit, or at least clear a suspect off my list. Well, that, and tell Nancy to ensure the news would get around town.

Despite my still somewhat-grim circumstances, things were looking up, at least a little, and I couldn't help but smile as I passed Rustic Treasures' Halloween decorations. The jack-o'-lanterns grinned at me with their mismatched expressions.

The wreath hanging on the wooden door of Blossom Boutique clattered as a gust of wind picked up, and I shivered. I should've brought a jacket. With the wind biting at me, I didn't give myself time to stop and admire the adorable miniature broomsticks and ceramic pumpkin vases displayed in the window before stepping inside, though I was careful to stay near the door in case I needed to make a break for it.

The scent of flowers assaulted me, trying to lure me into a false sense of security. The sweet, fruity fragrance of lilacs. The earthy smell with hints of floral that signified fresh lavender. And the almost citrusy scent with a hint of honeyed sweetness drifting from the roses. It was all a trap.

I pushed away General Ackbar's voice in my head. "Hello?"

The older lady I'd seen through the window moments before was nowhere in sight.

"Coming, coming." A door against the back wall opened, and Mr. Humphrey walked into view, leaning heavily on a cane. *Step. Step. Thump. Step. Step. Thump.*

With a walk that loud, it would've been difficult to sneak up on anyone. As long as he wasn't faking it.

I studied him as he approached with slow, deliberate movements. He wore a plain button-down shirt, brown slacks, and a simple cardigan draped over his shoulders. Was the feeble walk an act? The way he leaned on the cane for support *appeared* real. Considering how his thin wispy hair clung to his scalp, barely concealing the age spots and fine wrinkles etched into his skin, he had an impressive amount of hair on his face.

"How can I help you? Are you looking for something specific?" he asked as he finally came to a stop in front of me with his gnarled hands resting on the head of his cane. The slight stoop in his back, which I hadn't noticed when he'd been sitting in Nancy's bakery, was much more obvious now that he was standing.

"How about something that would go well in my bookshop?" I tried to come up with something on the spot.

"Your bookshop?" He raised one bushy eyebrow.

Could everyone do that but me? "I'm the owner of Whispering Pages." Well, not quite the owner, but I didn't know a good way to say it.

"You're Bettye's granddaughter?" He led me to a collection of plants against the far wall.

I nodded, and guilt twisted in my stomach for suspecting such a sweet old man, but I didn't have any other leads. Not that having a Santa Claus beard meant he couldn't commit murder, but it definitely made it harder to believe.

"So Marty's body was found in your shop, eh?" He stroked a plant's long leaves and separated two that were intertwining. "He got what he deserved, the greedy bastard." A savage glint replaced the twinkle in his blue eyes.

I leaned back. Mr. Humphrey was like Jekyll and Hyde—or Cooper and Sebastian. "So you know what happened?"

"Of course I do." He leaned on the counter and rested his cane against the display. "I went to Boston for a few days, not Timbuktu."

I blinked, then cleared my throat, trying to collect myself. "Word on the street is that you and Mr. James had quite the rivalry."

"It's true." He shrugged. "But now that he's gone, I don't have to worry so much."

That sounded like motive to me, but why would he admit so much? "And . . . you aren't worried about anyone suspecting you of his mur-der? I almost had a heart attack when the sheriff questioned me."

Mr. Humphrey barked out a laugh. "Suspect me? Whatever for? I wasn't even around that night. One of my granddaughters has been sick, so I went over to help."

"After you left your shop at eight?" I asked, then bit my lip. Maybe I shouldn't have revealed that.

He shifted his gaze to me, and despite the wrinkles at the edge of his eyes, it was still quite piercing. "You've been looking into me?"

"I might've swung by the other day," I said, unsure if I should be going with the innocent approach or admit it head-on. "I was hoping to talk to you then, but you were gone."

His intense stare continued for a few more seconds, and I fidgeted.

He laughed. "You think I murdered him, and you still came to ask me yourself? I'm not sure if you're brave or stupid or both, but either way, you've got chutzpah, and I like that."

"Um, thanks?" I let out a breath and released my phone, which I hadn't even realized I'd pulled from my pocket.

Mr. Humphrey shrugged as if apologizing for not being the murderer. "Sorry to disappoint you," he said with a small smile.

"You didn't," I said. "I'm glad I'm not sitting here talking to a murderer, but now I'm not totally sure what to do. There are still a lot of rumors going around, and I was hoping to shut them down."

"Let me guess, it's hurting business?"

I sighed and nodded. If it wasn't Mr. Humphrey, who else had a reason to want Mr. James dead? Well, the man was buying or already owned half of Main Street, and he was insufferable, so the list was probably really long. The trick would be narrowing down that list.

"I've got cameras inside and outside the shop that might help. I gave the police the surveillance footage, but I should have a backup copy on my computer." He gestured with his cane to a camera in the ceiling I hadn't noticed. "If you'd like, I could let you look through them. One faces Main," he said.

"Really?"

"No guarantee you'll see anything useful, but since our shops are only a few buildings away from each other, you might see *something* useful."

"I'd love that. Thank you!"

"We shop owners have to take care of each other." He led me between two rows of large plants with wide leaves to the back room, his cane heavy on the wooden floor.

Step. Step. Thump.

"Can I ask you something personal?" I asked as we made it to the back door.

"You came here to accuse me of murder and are now worrying about niceties?" He shook his head, but he was smiling. "Go ahead."

I flushed but pressed on. "If you own a good portion of the town, why do you work in this little flower shop?"

He was silent for a long moment. "Because it belonged to my wife," he said in a soft voice. "And keeping these flowers alive and seeing the joy they bring people is my way of keeping her memory alive too."

My throat tightened at his obvious love. "How long has she been gone?"

"Ten years now." He sighed and pointed to a computer. "My son hooked it up so I can watch all the security footage. Let me sign in for you, and I'll let you go through the stuff from that night."

"Thanks again. This means a lot to me."

"I know what it's like to struggle with a new business. I wasn't always as well off as I am now." He fired up the computer and typed in a password using his pointer finger. A few minutes later, he had the program up. "Seeing as you're at least four decades younger than me,

I'm sure you're tech savvy enough to figure this out, but holler if you need help. I'd better get back to trimming the thorns from my roses if I'm going to finish a few more arrangements tonight."

"Thank you." I didn't look away from the screen as I clicked on the video from five days ago and scooted the bar along the bottom of the screen until I was seeing the footage from around six that night. I set it to play at double speed so it wouldn't take so long, my finger hovering over the pause button in case I saw something.

It showed a good amount of Main Street, but only a partial image of my front door. With it being the night of the festival, the street was packed. I skimmed through the video. I'd gone back to the shop around seven thirty to collect Nana's money, and the note hadn't been there yet. While the police had given me a window of nine to midnight, I wanted to make sure, so I started watching from the moment I returned to the shop.

I shuddered at the thought of his dead body lying in the darkness of my store as I stood on the street, reading the note from him the next morning. As I watched myself open the door on the video and rubbed away the goosebumps on my arms as I imagined the murderer hanging around. I shook my head and focused on the screen, pulling my wandering thoughts back to the moment's task. The video sped by in a blur of black and white.

There was Mr. Humphrey, leaving the shop and getting into his car around eight fifteen, like he said. A few pedestrians walked down the street. A mom and her little girl. A family eating caramel apples on a stick from the festival. A teenager on a bike. A man in a suit.

I stopped the camera and stared at the pixelated version of Mr. James, then I looked at the time stamp. He was still alive at nine thirty and was heading toward my shop. He stopped at the door and pulled something from his pocket—probably the notice about rent. As he started to put it on the door, he stopped and looked through the glass.

What was he looking at?

The door to Whispering Pages opened. From the inside.

Finger trembling, I pressed the space bar and let the video continue.

The door opened wider, and Mr. James stepped inside, talking to someone. The paper in his hand fluttered to the ground as he disappeared into the darkness. The video kept playing, but one thought looped in my mind like a broken feed. It wasn't Mr. James who had let himself into Whispering Pages; someone else had already been inside.

If I was going to find the murderer or Nana's missing money, I had to find out who else had a key to Nana's shop.

Chapter 10

One Step Closer

I watched the video, waiting for the killer to emerge, until the time stamp read midnight, but they never did—at least not from the front door of Whispering Pages. Then I watched it again. And again. Did they know about the camera, or had they just assumed it'd be better to stay off Main Street so they left through the back door?

Leaning back in the chair, I stared at the brick wall and chewed on my thumbnail. Whoever had killed Mr. James had access to Whispering Pages, even though I should be the only one with a key, besides Mr. James. I needed to change the locks at Whispering Pages. The thought that a killer had access to my shop made me shiver.

My trip to Blossom Boutique had eliminated one suspect and added another. Despite Lillian's story, I still wasn't convinced she wasn't involved. Plus, I'd gained a vital clue from the video. Now I needed to figure out what to do with it. Also, I needed to change the locks at Whispering Pages.

The door opened, and Lillian walked in, balancing a large plant on her hip. When she saw me, she stopped, her eyes widening. "I didn't know anyone was back here."

"Your father let me in so I could watch some footage from the night of the festival." I closed out of the program as I stood and turned to face her.

"I see." She bustled to the side and put the plant down, then started looking through boxes with her back to me.

If she was guilty, she sure was good at acting innocent. Maybe I'd need to press harder.

I rested an elbow on the armrest, trying to appear nonchalant. "You didn't mention that Mr. Humphrey was your father when I asked about him."

She laughed and turned, now holding a beautiful glass vase. "Most everyone in town already knows we're related. I forgot you were new."

She forgot I was new? When I'd gotten nothing but curious glances and notoriety since the murder. Maybe it was time for a different approach. I pulled the paper with the flower design on it from my purse and held it out to her. "Do you recognize this?"

She glanced at it on her way to the door. "Of course."

I followed her out, still searching for some sort of reaction. She'd admitted to it so easily. Did she really have no idea what it was for, or was she tricking me by playing it cool? "I found it in my shop the day Mr. James was murdered." Technically, I found it a few hours before he was killed, but I needed to see if she'd have a reaction.

And there it was.

Her eyes widened, and she stopped. "You did?" She seemed to pull herself together and kept walking. "That isn't too unusual, I suppose."

"You don't think it is?" I watched as she took the vase to the back wall and started a new arrangement of fall flowers. She was as hard to read as Sebastian.

"Not really." She gestured over her shoulder toward the front desk. "I pass those papers out to almost anyone who comes into the shop for promotional purposes. Anyone who'd been in here could've had one and dropped it in your bookshop."

"Oh, I see." If she was telling the truth—and the stack of papers by the register seemed to support her story—then I'd reached a dead end with the money case.

My phone beeped a reminder at me, and I jumped. It was time for dinner with María. "Well, thank you for your time. I'd better go." I grabbed my bag and headed for the door, nodding toward Mr. Humphrey, who was helping a customer.

"Wait," Lillian called after me as I reached the entrance.

"Yes?"

She pursed her lips. "I update the design every once in a while to keep things fresh, so I can tell you that whoever had that paper had come in here within the last two weeks."

"That's the last time you changed it?" My heart started pounding, and when she nodded, I added, "Do you have a list of customers I could look at?" There was always the chance that the person might've come in and not ended up in her book, but at least it gave me a place to start.

"I do, but . . ."

"Their names would be enough. I don't need any other information," I said at her hesitation. "Please, this is to help me find something of my grandmother's that was stolen."

Her expression softened. "Well, if it's for Bettye." She led me to a large book lying near the register. "I record every transaction in here."

"Can I take pictures of the last two weeks? I don't have time to go through it all now."

"Sure." She folded the page so only the names and dates of the transactions were visible.

I snapped a few photos while she watched. Then she closed the book.

"Seriously, thank you so much," I said.

"You're welcome. Anything to help Bettye's granddaughter."

Once outside, crisp air blew down the street, carrying the earthy scent of autumn leaves and the distant aroma of freshly baked pies. I inhaled, letting the ordinary smells ground me while I thought over what I'd learned.

If Mr. Humphrey had an alibi, and Lillian had an explanation for the paper, then where did that leave me? Maybe the answer would be somewhere in the pictures I'd taken.

"What's the long face for, Harpsy?"

I spun around and found Cooper walking down the street behind me, his long legs closing the distance between us. He shot me a brilliant smile, and I couldn't help but return it.

"Just a little stressed about work and stuff." There wasn't much reason to talk to Cooper about it. He'd moved to Whisper Hollow a few years before me and probably didn't know the intricacies of the town like Nancy did.

"You shouldn't let it stress you out," he said as he caught up to me. "It'll ruin that pretty face of yours."

"You are unbelievable." I rolled my eyes but also couldn't help but smile. My heart leaped at his compliment. "Is there anyone in this town you haven't flirted with?"

He glanced behind me toward Blossom Boutique. "I'm not sure I've had the pleasure with Mr. Humphrey . . . yet."

"You're something else, you know that?"

Cooper leaned close and winked at me. "Half the reason I do it is to annoy Seb. It's to pay him back for being so annoyingly overprotective all the time."

"And the other half?"

"Because it's fun," he said as we crossed to the other side of Main. "Anyway, you going back to work?"

"No, I'm going to Nancy's to meet a friend for dinner."

"A friend, huh?" He raised a dark eyebrow. "It wouldn't be a guy, would it?"

I laughed, and small butterflies took flight in my stomach at his slightly jealous tone. "Definitely not."

"Definitely?" Now the other eyebrow rose to join the first. "Do you lack confidence in guys or in yourself?"

"Guys—I've sworn off dating," I admitted as we reached the front door to Sugarplum Delights.

Cooper leaned close and opened the door for me, his warm breath tickling my ear as he said, "Now *that* sounds like a challenge if I've ever heard one."

I flushed and stepped away from him, taking one step into the store. "It wasn't."

"We'll see about that. See ya later, Harper." He flashed another brilliant smile at me, then sauntered down the street.

A moment later, María pulled me through the entry and into the inviting aroma of pumpkin spice. "Were you flirting with Cooper Moore?" The hum of conversation, punctuated by bursts of laughter and the occasional clatter of dishes, threatened to drown out her words.

"More like he was flirting with me." Heat rose to my cheeks, and I glanced at her. "Actually, that sounded super full of myself. I meant—"

"That Cooper loves to flirt. I know." Still, she looked down the street after him and sighed. "Even still, I'd date him in a heartbeat."

"He's got looks and charm, that's for sure." I said as we moved to the long line to place our orders.

"He isn't the type to commit, which is why we only went on two dates."

"Sounds about right." Yet another difference from Tate. He was all too willing to commit. *Staying* committed was another matter entirely.

"Don't get me wrong," María said. "Cooper is great, but he dates a bit too much. As opposed to his brother, who doesn't date at all."

"Sebastian isn't dating anyone?" I asked a bit too quickly. Despite his surly nature, he was attractive and, apparently, kind-hearted.

"I don't think he's dated anyone since he moved here."

"Probably because he's so reticent." Though he did have the sexy nerd thing going for him.

She laughed and wiggled her eyebrows. "There are plenty of other things to do besides talk," she said. "But it's a shame. I know quite a few women around town who would volunteer to go out with him if he gave them the chance."

"I'll admit, it's hard to imagine him dating someone."

"Are you saying you wouldn't date him in a heartbeat?"

More like he'd never date me, but he seemed like he'd be a good boyfriend. I couldn't picture Sebastian ever cheating on anyone, but all I said was, "I don't think we'd work together."

"Hmm," María said as we made it to the front of the line and placed our orders with a flustered Nancy. Her gray-streaked hair, pulled back in a loose bun, was escaping in unruly tendrils, and she had a pencil tucked behind one ear.

"Everything okay?" I asked.

"Yeah, just a little overbooked and understaffed tonight." She fanned a hand around her flushed face. "A small tour group came through at the same time as the dinner rush, and as you can see, it's madness."

Behind the counter, the brass espresso machine hissed and sputtered, sending out the rich, comforting scent of freshly brewed coffee.

"Anything I can do to help?" I asked.

Nancy smiled and pushed a loose curl behind her ear. "I'll be all right. You enjoy your food."

We placed our orders—I decided to try something new—and stepped back to let the people behind us order. Guess my questions would have to wait until the next time I stopped in. Nancy was far too busy for me to talk to her about anything.

About ten minutes later, Nancy placed a platter loaded with steaming bowls of pumpkin soup, roasted turkey sandwiches with cranberry sauce, and mashed potatoes and gravy in front of us. A few droplets of gravy had made their way onto her uniform, but she didn't seem to notice.

"Thanks," I told her as we collected our food. During the next half hour, we busied ourselves with devouring the scrumptious meal while I asked María more questions about Whisper Hollow. Maybe she'd have some insight into how things were when Nana was still alive.

"So did you go to Whispering Pages much when my nana ran it?" I asked between sips of the creamy pumpkin soup. The soup had a savory-sweet flavor with earthy and mildly nutty undertones. I took another bite, enjoying the crunch of the onions, leeks, and garlic that contrasted with the soup's smooth velvety texture.

"Not really," she said. "My mom would when she was practicing English, but I didn't go with her much." She shrugged and gave me a rueful grin. Her smile was beautiful against her dark skin. "It had a different feel before you came."

I covered my regret with a smile. If María hadn't come around much, she probably didn't know who Nana had been close to—whom she would have given a key to the shop. Then I frowned. I was assuming that Nana *had* given the key out, but what if someone had stolen it?

Before my thoughts could run away with me and the lull in the conversation got too long, I cleared my throat. "You said your mom was practicing English, right? What is her native language?"

"Spanish." With well-manicured hands, María smoothed a wrinkle from the plaid tablecloth. "She grew up in Mexico City."

My eyes widened, and I couldn't help but look at her with a touch of envy. "Wow. That's cool. I wish I knew another language."

"It's never too late to start. I bet you could pick up Spanish in no time."

"Maybe I will, once I get my business back on its feet."

The restaurant hummed with the chatter of patrons, the clinking of cutlery, and the aroma of Nancy's cooking. For a moment, I could almost pretend that everything was fine.

María grabbed my hand across the table, a smile lighting up her face. "I just got the best idea."

"About what?"

"About Whispering Pages," she said. "You should host a Halloween party there! You've already got most of the decorations. It'd be perfect. We can capitalize on everyone's morbid curiosity."

"That could be a good idea," I said slowly.

María let go of my hand and took another bite of her soup. Her dark eyes glittered with excitement. "A good idea? No, it's great. This is the perfect way to get people into the shop and show them how cool it is. From there, it's only one more step to get them buying books."

"True."

"If you want, I'll help you plan it."

"That's nice of you."

"Not really," she said. "I love any excuse to plan a party."

I let the idea simmer while I asked María more about her family and Whisper Hollow, trying to get a feel for what to expect the rest of my life to look like if I decided to stay. Town festivals, small business problems, newcomers like me stirring up a buzz in town. It was a far cry from Phoenix, but a quiet, uneventful life was what I needed after the Tate drama.

Too bad my first two weeks at Whisper Hollow had been anything but uneventful. But if I could figure out who was behind Mr. James's murder and Nana's missing money, then maybe I'd get the quiet life I needed. Which meant I needed to get home and look through those photos from the flower shop to see if I could find a connection to the two cases somehow.

We talked until half past eight, then said our goodbyes outside the restaurant. I walked to the alley to grab my bike. Someone had woven lights around the lamp posts lining Main Street, and they twinkled like orange stars on the empty street, but the alley was dark. With Main Street quiet except for the occasional car passing by, my footsteps sounded louder than usual in the alley.

Now that I was alone again, I couldn't help but think about how the murderer had probably been in that very alley after killing Mr. James. My hands trembled as I fumbled with my bike lock, and I scanned the darkness for threats. The building loomed on either side of me, but I couldn't make out much else. The hairs on the back of my neck prickled with unease.

Ahead of me, something rustled.

I froze, my heart thumping wildly. The security of Main Street felt miles away instead of yards.

"Hello?" I called out in a trembling voice.

No one answered.

A chill breeze raced down the alley, stirring the piles of dry leaves along the wall. A dead leaf cracked as someone stepped on it.

My heart jumped to my throat, and my pulse took off.

I wasn't alone.

Chapter 11

Clockwork Chemistry

"Who's there?" I called into the darkness, but the fear clawing at my chest stole my volume so the words were barely more than a whisper.

Silence answered.

Something glinted at me from several feet away.

With shaking hands, I tried, again, to unlock my bike. My heartbeat thudded in my ears. After a few more heart-throttling seconds, I got the key in and turned it. My lock clattered to the ground.

The noise echoed in the alley.

No, that wasn't an echo. Something else was making noise in the darkness.

A hollow clang sounded, as if someone had bumped into one of the metal trash cans.

I whipped out my phone and turned on the flashlight before dialing 9-1-1, but I didn't hit the button. "I'll call the police," I called out in a still-wavering voice as I swept my flashlight across the narrow alley. Nothing but some metal trash cans, a few wooden crates, and piles of leaves. A broken scarecrow with polished button eyes leaned against the wall. Was that what I'd seen? With a self-deprecating laugh, I tried to shake off my unease, but my heart still pounded.

Something wrapped around my ankles.

I dropped my phone, which landed on something that hissed.

"Jiji?" I asked with my heart in my throat.

She glared up at me.

Holding a hand to my heart, I leaned against the side of the building and slid to my butt.

Jiji, apparently forgiving me for dropping my phone on her and taking my sitting down as an invitation, settled into my lap with a satisfied purr.

"You are the worst." I petted her for a second until my hands weren't trembling as much, then I collected my phone and the dropped bike lock, put Jiji in the basket, and wheeled the bike onto Main Street. Before hopping on, I shoved an AirPod into my ear and wrapped my scarf around my nose to counter the chill.

A hand descended onto my shoulder. I screamed and whirled around.

Sebastian stepped back and held his hands up in front of him, watching me with wide eyes.

"Oh my gosh." I held a hand to my heart. "You about gave me a heart attack. What are you doing?"

He ducked his head. Strands of hair peeked out from beneath his charcoal-gray beanie. "Sorry. I saw you put your headphones in and didn't think you'd hear if I called out. I wanted to see if you were okay. You seemed troubled when you wheeled your bike out."

"Yeah, I'm a little jumpy. Jiji surprised me in the alley."

Speak of the devil, she meowed and hopped from the basket to wrap herself around Sebastian's legs. Shameless cat.

"So you're okay?" He gave me a searching look.

"Yeah." I slowly exhaled to calm my racing heart and looked up at him. I'd kill for long eyelashes like his—maybe too soon to joke about killing. "I've been meaning to thank you."

"For what?" He raised an eyebrow—he and Cooper were so similar in some ways, yet still so different.

"For talking to the sheriff and giving me an alibi, and for coming by that night to return that book."

"That was nothing." He shrugged and looked down at Jiji.

Was it the glow from the streetlamps, or did his cheeks look red? "Why didn't you tell me you stopped by that night?"

He rubbed the back of his neck. "I guess I didn't want it to seem weird, but when I found that book from the shop, I remembered I needed to swing by and greet Bettye's family, but when I did, I saw that you were asleep, so I just put it on the porch and left."

"Well, thanks again."

"Do you know if the police have had any luck finding a suspect?"

"I'm not sure." I tended to avoid Sheriff Warner.

"I hope they find them soon," he said.

"Me too."

A few seconds passed, and my heartbeat started to pound for a different reason. I wasn't used to being alone with Sebastian.

"Well, I'd better go. Early morning tomorrow." He spun around and walked away before I could say anything.

I watched him for a moment, relief and disappointment flickering through me, before hopping on my bike and pedaling down Main. My heart still raced from my jump scare in the alley, but not as badly after seeing Sebastian. His presence had been strangely reassuring, especially after thinking I was about to be attacked by a killer. I smiled as I realized, for once, we'd had a pretty decent interaction that hadn't left either of us in a bad mood or injured.

"Hey Siri, call Grace," I said into my AirPod. The chill wind whipped my hair behind me and nipped at my face and hands. Jiji meowed and tucked herself low into the basket.

"Calling Grace," Siri responded in a sexy British tone that always made me think of James Bond. But even that wasn't enough to calm me.

The phone rang a few times, then Grace picked up. "What's up?"

"Biking home."

Grace sighed. "I wish you'd quit doing that. I hate the thought of you biking around town by yourself when the mur—person is still out there."

The fact that she'd edited herself told me her kids were nearby, though I couldn't hear them at the moment.

"I know. You're right. Maybe I'll drive tomorrow." Considering how much I'd overreacted about Jiji, it was probably best for the next little bit. I left Main Street behind and coasted down the hill. The moon, a pale crescent, hung low in the sky and cast a faint silvery glow over the road.

"Wow. What happened? You never give in so easily."

I forced a laugh. "Nothing. Oh, actually, something good happened today."

"What?"

"Sheriff Warner came by and told me I'm off the hook."

"What?" That time the word came out as a screech. "That's fantastic. How?"

I spent the next ten minutes of my bike ride explaining how Sebastian had swung by during the festival to drop off a book and provided my alibi and also about my conversation with Lillian.

"Wow. A real knight in shining armor, huh? Maybe he'll be the one to break the curse," she teased.

"Don't be silly. There is no curse."

"What else do you call five failed relationships in a row with guys who all ended up being total douches?"

"A string of terrible luck," I said as I parked my bike on the porch and unlocked the front door. "And that's not fair, Todd and I weren't even dating, so that shouldn't count."

"Because he ghosted you before it even got that far!"

I stepped inside, letting Jiji follow me in before I closed and locked the door. It felt good to be home. "*Anyway,* that's not all that happened today. I also visited Mr. Humphrey. Turns out he isn't the murderer."

"Maybe it's better that way," Grace said. "I don't love the idea of you playing the amateur sleuth and hunting down whoever did it."

"Well . . ."

"Uh oh. I know that tone. Well, what?"

"While watching his security footage, I saw Mr. James enter Whispering Pages on the night he was murdered."

"So he had a key?"

I knelt in front of the fireplace and arranged some of the kindling before striking a match. I had a chill I couldn't shake. "That's the thing; the door opened . . . from the inside."

"You're saying someone else has a key to your shop?"

"Yup." I suppressed a shudder and leaned back to look at the fireplace decorations. The twinkling fairy lights decorating the mantel were set on a timer so the house felt a little less empty when I came home from work, but sometimes they gave a weird glow to hand-painted ceramic jack-o'-lanterns, turning their friendly grins eerie.

"You have to find out who. Whoever it is, we can assume that's the culprit."

"I thought you were against me chasing down murderers?" I teased as I placed two small logs over the kindling.

"I am, but I'm more against that person having access to you in the shop anytime they want."

"I'll go to the bank tomorrow. Maybe they have a record of whom else might have a copy," I said. "Plus, I've already got an appointment set to get the locks changed."

Jiji came and wrapped around my legs with a happy purr. She enjoyed fires as much as I did—in a non-pyro way, of course.

"It also might be worth it to look through Nana's things. Maybe she left some sort of clue behind that could help you figure out who she would've trusted enough to give a key."

"Good idea," I said. "I also got a few pictures from Lillian of the list of customers who visited the flower shop over the last few weeks, since part of one of their fliers, instead of Nana's money, was inside *Inkheart*."

"Feels like a long shot, but I guess it's better than nothing." Grace inhaled sharply. "Harp, I realized something."

"What?" I zoomed in on the photos and tried to read Lillian's spidery scrawl.

"We already know two people Nana might've given a key to her shop."

"We do?" I readjusted a log on the fire so it wouldn't smother and go out before returning my attention to the pictures again. "Who?"

"Cooper and Sebastian."

I laughed. "You think one of them had something to do with all of this? I can't picture them hurting a fly." Flirting with one maybe, in

Cooper's case. "Plus, they seemed to care for Nana. How could they steal from her?"

"I'm not saying they did, but you've got to admit that Nana talked about them an awful lot. Even if they don't have a key themselves, they might know someone who does."

"True," I said. "I suppose there's no harm in talking to them."

"Be casual and see if they got a key from Nana or if they knew who might have."

"Okay, I will." Butterflies fluttered in my stomach at the thought of talking to them. No, not butterflies. Nerves. It had nothing to do with the thought of seeing Sebastian again. Nothing at all. I glared down at my phone while I tried to get a handle on my emotions. But then a name jumped out at me from the screen.

"Oh no," I whispered as I read the list of names.

"What's wrong?"

"Maybe you're right after all." I held the phone tighter in my shaking hand to make sure I wasn't mistaken. "I found Sebastian's name on the list."

~

The next morning, instead of biking, I drove my car into town. After a quick appointment to get the locks changed at Whispering Pages, I slid my Prius into one of the few spaces in front of my shop. If we did have a party, we'd have to figure out parking. Finding spots on Main Street was often a nightmare.

I walked next door to Grain and Glass. Sebastian and Cooper couldn't be involved, but I had to clear their names off my list, just to be sure. After finding Sebastian's name on the flower shop's list, I'd spent a good hour reading old emails from Nana, and in more than one, she'd mentioned the brothers helping her with projects around the shop. According to her, they could do no wrong, and it sounded like they'd helped her with projects all the time. It wouldn't be odd at all for them to have a key, like Grace had suggested.

Had I let my growing friendship with the brothers cloud my judgment? Considering how much work they did with their hands, it wouldn't be unusual for them to have a set of tools. Then again, almost everyone owned a hammer. Either way, now was my chance to get some answers.

"Hello?" I called as I walked through the front door into an empty room.

"Be right there," Sebastian's smooth baritone answered from the back.

My stomach tightened with nerves. I tried to channel the energy into movement by walking the perimeter of the room. And though I should've been practicing what I'd decided to say to Sebastian, some of their pieces caught my eye. I ran a finger over the smooth dark wood of a jewelry box polished to perfection and meticulously crafted with intricate inlays. It sat open, showcasing glass bead necklaces, bracelets, and earrings with vivid, swirling colors.

With Cooper making the glass items and Sebastian the wood, they were an amazing team. No wonder their business seemed to be doing well.

I shook my head and tucked my hands behind my back to keep from touching anything else. I really needed to focus on the upcoming conversation, not the adorable collection of tiny glass cats, scarecrows, cauldrons, and other Halloween-themed items. Coming to a stop in front of a gorgeous wooden grandfather clock, I ran through my prepared lines like some sort of actor in a murder drama. I needed to be collected and cool. Vague but decisive.

"Sorry to have kept you waiting."

I spun around to face Sebastian as he walked out of the back room. His tousled dark hair fell across his forehead, a hint of wood shavings dusting his thick locks.

"What can I do—" He looked up from the rag he was using to wipe his hands, and his eyes widened.

I shoved my hands into my pockets and tried not to admire how his well-fitted flannel shirt showed off his broad shoulders. "Hi."

"Oh, hey." He cleared his throat but didn't say anything else.

"Not one for decorating for the holidays, are you?" I shifted my weight from foot to foot.

He looked around his shop as if seeing it for the first time. "No."

His strained tone urged me not to pry further, so instead, I pointed to the tiny glass decorations I'd admired earlier. "What about those?"

"Coop makes them," he said. "Seasonal items sell well."

"And that?" I gestured to the small, crocheted pumpkin sitting near the register.

He smiled. "Your grandmother made that for us the year we opened Grain and Glass. She said the shop was too dreary and needed a woman's touch."

"That sounds like Nana." I laughed. "She couldn't resist decorating things. You should see her house, er, my house."

"You better be careful," Sebastian said. "If you'd said that to Coop, he would've taken it as an invitation to stop by."

I looked down. Hopefully, he couldn't see the flush traveling down my neck.

The ghost of a smile crossed his face, making his blue eyes sparkle. I didn't get to see him smile much. His lips looked firm but inviting.

"See something you like?"

"Yes."

At his raised eyebrow, I realized I was still staring at him. I flushed and pointed to the clock. "I love this." I reached out to touch the clock's smooth wood. I was acting like I'd never seen an attractive man before—and also like I'd forgotten that I'd come to ascertain whether he'd killed my landlord.

"Yeah, she's a beaut." Sebastian's eyes lit with enthusiasm, and he stepped closer, bringing the scent of earth and pine with him. He stroked its front, leaving our hands a few inches apart. "The walnut makes a warm foundation for the clock, and the dark ebony of the stem adds a touch of elegance. I got my hands on some rare burl wood for the dial, and it's—" He cut himself off and dropped his hand as the tips of his ears turned red. "Sorry."

I smiled. "It's fun to hear about your passion." Seeing how much he loved it almost made me want to buy the clock, especially after Jiji delayed his last project. Not that I should be spending extra money after paying for new locks. "I'm sorry again, by the way, about what happened with Jiji a few days ago. I hope your delivery went well."

"It did. Thank you." His expression warmed as he turned back to the clock. It was obvious how much he loved woodworking.

I shook my head. I hadn't come to learn more about Sebastian. Well, I had, but not about his passions.

"I was wondering if I could ask you a question."

"Okay, shoot."

"It seems like my grandmother was fond of you and Cooper," I started.

"We were fond of her too."

I swallowed past the lump in my throat. The pain in his dark gaze brought back an echo of loneliness that had wrapped around me like a dark shroud at Nana's passing. "Thank you for everything you did for her," I whispered.

"She did as much for us." He clasped his hands behind his back. "When we moved here, she took us under her wing. She practically adopted us, and after"—he swallowed and shook his head—"anyway, I owe her a lot. I'm grateful for her and for the life Coop and I have managed to build here. Things weren't the best before we moved."

"I still can't believe she's gone," I whispered. "Between losing her, almost losing the shop, and now the stuff with Mr. James . . . everything has been so crazy."

Sebastian put a large warm hand on my shoulder. "I'm sure things will get better soon."

I stiffened, my nerve endings firing at his touch. "Did she ever give you and Cooper a key to Whispering Pages?" I blurted, then winced. That wasn't at all how I'd planned on asking, but his touch had frazzled me.

"Yes, we had a key." He rubbed his chin.

My breath caught at the admission. They had one. And Sebastian's name was on that list.

"But when your grandmother decided she was going to leave you the shop, we returned it. If you check the bottom drawer in her office, I'm sure you'll find it. Why? Did you lose yours?"

"No. I've been curious how many people have access to the shop besides Mr. James and me. I wanted to rule you two out as suspects."

"Suspects?" The softness fell from Sebastian's expression like autumn leaves abandoning the trees. He lost the laugh lines around his eyes, and his face fell into hard lines.

"Well, more like . . ." I floundered for a better way to say it but came up short.

He scowled at me. "And if you'd bothered to listen, you'd also know that both Coop and I have alibis. We were at the festival that night."

Well, not all night since he'd come to my house to return the book, but they probably had more people accounting for their whereabouts than I did. Had Tate made me suspicious of men? How could I have even thought of accusing either of the brothers when it was clear they loved Nana so much? But then again, loving Nana didn't mean anything when it came to Mr. James's murder—unless the missing money was connected.

Tension in my stomach deflated. "I see."

"Now if you're done flinging wild accusations, I need to get back to work." He walked to the door and held it open for me.

"Sebastian, I'm sorry. I . . ." I trailed off, unsure of how to make it right. So much for our decent interaction the other night. Would we ever be able to talk without ending up in an argument?

Chapter 12

Not All Dead Ends Lead to Disappointment

I closed the front door of Whispering Pages and leaned against it with a sigh. "I messed up."

"What do you mean?" Grace's voice was calming through my Air-Pod.

I told her about what happened next door versus how I'd planned for it to go, ending with, "and when I checked Nana's office, the key was exactly where he said it would be." My stomach twisted as I remembered the look on his face. Not that we had much of a relationship to ruin—even if I wanted one—but I was pretty sure that accusing an innocent person of murder counted as burning a bridge. "I think Tate ruined me."

"He did *not* ruin you," she said. "He doesn't have that sort of power over you."

I paced around the shop while Jiji meowed at me from the top of a romance shelf. "Yes, he does. I never would've been so quick to judge Sebastian if Tate hadn't ruined my trust in the male species."

"You didn't doubt him because he's a guy. You doubted him because he was a logical suspect based on clues you found."

"I should probably give up on this whole amateur detective thing." I sighed. "I suck at it."

"That's not true. You followed a lead, and it didn't take you where you needed to go," she said. "According to every detective novel I've ever read, that isn't unusual."

"Yes, because I'm sure my life is going to play out like a mystery novel." I flipped my hair over my shoulder.

"You never know."

"Maybe I'm better off leaving town." I sank into a comfy armchair tucked between shelves and put my head in my hands. "I'm not sure why I thought I could do this anyway, with Nana's shop or the murder and the money."

Grace was silent for a moment. "You *could* come home."

"But?" I asked. Because with that tone of voice, there was always a *but*.

"But I don't think it's a good idea."

"Why not? You were ready to drag me back a few days ago."

Her voice softened. "That was because I was worried about you, not because you were giving up."

"I'm not giving up. I'm just . . ." Proving that the sheriff and Mr. James were right about me all along.

"Harp, listen to me," Grace said. "I am all for you coming back and staying with us until they find whoever is responsible and put him or her behind bars. But that doesn't mean I think you should give up on Whispering Pages."

"But what if I fail?" I whispered.

"Then you fail."

I blinked. That wasn't exactly the answer, or comfort, I'd expected. "Gee, thanks."

"You're acting like failure is a bad thing." She laughed. "Logan, can you tell Aunt Harp what we say about failure in our house?"

Static sounded through the phone as it changed hands, then a tiny three-year-old voice came through the speaker. "Thuccess ith built on a foundation of faiwures."

"Thanks, Logan." I couldn't help but smile at his piece of wisdom and adorable lisp.

Noises sounded again, then Grace came back on. "Plus, you know what Dad always says."

"Bloom where you're planted." I sighed again. Grace always seemed to know the right thing to say. But, more importantly, she wasn't afraid to say it, even when it wasn't what I wanted to hear.

"Seriously, you're welcome to come here until things settle down."

I shook my head. "I can't leave the shop for that long if I'm going to keep it alive. I have two weeks to get the money for the bank."

"If you're worried about the rent—"

"No, Grace. I'm not taking your money. If I'm going to succeed with this, I'm going to do it myself." I turned to stare out the front window as a flash of pink walked by. It was Nancy, probably on her way to Sugarplum Delights. "I'd better go. I have another clue to find."

"Okay, I'll talk to you later. Call whenever."

Almost as soon as we disconnected, my phone buzzed in my pocket. I pulled it out with a smile. Had Grace remembered something else?

My hand tightened around the phone as I read the message, and my smile fell.

Harp, I'm serious. We need to talk. I'm sorry about what happened. I made a mistake, but things are over with her. I miss you. Call me back.

The words plucked at my heart's frayed edges, leaving it in a confused tangle. Tate couldn't honestly believe I'd forgive him after he cheated on me while we were engaged, could he? I mean, even if I could forgive him, that didn't mean I'd ever want to date him again. If I'd burned my bridge with Sebastian—the thought brought a pang of remorse—then Tate had blown his up with dynamite.

I shoved my cell back in my pocket and walked outside, flipping the sign over the door to *closed*. Hadn't Tate gotten the message when I didn't respond to his last text?

A brisk breeze blew down the street, tugging at my hair and cutting through my sweater. I shivered and walked the few steps to Nancy's bakery. As soon as I opened the door, the delicious aroma of pumpkin and cinnamon enveloped me like a warm hug.

"Morning, darlin'," Nancy called from behind the counter.

It was one of those rare moments when the shop was empty except for a cute old lady browsing the baked desserts at the front.

"Morning, Nancy. Where is everyone?"

"I decided to open a little late this morning, and I only just got back. Evelyn here was practically banging down my door."

The older woman laughed and swatted at Nancy with a wrinkled hand. "I was not." She glanced at me and whispered conspiratorially, "But sometimes a woman needs more than the crap they serve at the home."

"The home?" I asked.

"Evelyn lives at the assisted living place down the block—the one that's near the motel," Nancy said before turning to Evelyn. "Evelyn, I'd like you to meet Bettye's granddaughter."

Evelyn shook my hand with a bony, surprisingly strong grip. "We sure do miss her around here. She was a hoot."

I smiled. It was easy to imagine the three women strolling around town together like they owned the place. "I miss her too."

Evelyn accepted a cup from Nancy, then waved. "Well, I better get back. Nice to meet you, hun."

"You too." I waved at her as she slipped out the door, then turned back to Nancy. "It's unlike you to open late."

"I had a big order of cupcakes to drop off for a Halloween party in town." She left the counter to refresh some flowers in a few centerpieces on the tables, then straightened the plaid tablecloths.

Her words reminded me of María's party idea, and though it wasn't why I'd come, my head spun with possibilities. "Maybe I should hire you too."

"For what?"

"I'm thinking of hosting a Halloween party in the shop to attract more customers."

"I have great rates for bulk orders." She flashed me a smile and winked. "Plus, I can give you the new-to-town discount."

"Let me think about it and get back to you."

"Sounds good." She moved behind the counter again. "Give me a minute, and I'll whip up a new drink for you to try."

I moved to help her with the tables. "I was hoping to talk to you. I hadn't mentioned this yet, but Nana told me she left some money behind for me to use for the store."

"Oh? That was nice of her." Nancy smiled and started mixing a pumpkin spice drink, throwing in clove and cardamom.

"I didn't know about it until I read that letter you gave me, but when I went to get the money that night, it was gone."

"Gone?" Her eyes widened.

"Yeah, I thought maybe it was related to the murder, but now I'm not so sure."

She put the drink on the counter. "Why do you think it's related?"

I finished the last table and picked up the drink, letting it warm my hands through the paper cup. "Because they happened close together."

"Did they?" she asked. "Or did you assume that because Mr. James was killed the same night you discovered the money was missing?"

I mulled over her words. "I guess I might've jumped to conclusions, but I don't have any real reason to think they aren't related."

"But you also don't have any reason to think they are." She flashed a quick smile and erased the day's special from the chalkboard. "The money could have gone missing any time after Bettye's passing."

"You don't think they're connected?" I took a small sip.

Her hand slipped as she wrote Fall Quiche on the board. "I don't know. Maybe not."

Why was Nancy being weird? Or was I being too jumpy and suspicious? Trying to find the killer was wearing on my nerves.

"Anyway, have you made any progress with finding the money?" Nancy looked up and smiled, seeming normal again. It was all in my head.

"Not a ton." I summarized what I'd done, from my trip to the park and discovering Lillian's connection, to my conversation with Lillian, the photos, and the list with Sebastian's name on it.

"So you met the Lloyds at the park? Good, good. Nice family," she said. "I think Jessie is about your age too."

"Yes, she was nice."

"And you got to go back to Blossom Boutique." Nancy smiled. "That was one of Bettye's favorite places. She used to go every week to buy fresh flowers for the bookshop."

I frowned and squeezed my cup a little too tight, making a few drops of steaming liquid spill onto my hand. I winced and wiped at it with a napkin. "But I don't know what to do next, and now I'm stuck with both cases."

"I'm still not convinced they're connected. You thought Sebastian could be a killer because he bought some flowers?" Nancy tsked and shook her head. "That boy wouldn't harm a fly."

I debated correcting her use of the term *boy*, considering how good he'd looked an hour ago. He was definitely no boy.

"Chivalry isn't dead, Nancy. Mr. James is. And we have to figure out who did it," I said. "I was wrong about Sebastian, but the killer is still out there."

"Fair enough." She sighed. "I suppose this isn't some K-drama."

"I was wondering if you could think of anyone else whom Nana might've given a key."

"Hmm." She continued to bustle around the bakery. "I had a spare key to Whispering Pages once upon a time, but I'm not sure what I did with the darn thing." Her forehead wrinkled as she thought. "No one else comes to mind, but I'll keep thinking on it."

"Okay, thanks." My stomach sank. How many keys did Nana hand out? At this rate, the killer was going to get away with it. I could feel the case slipping away from me as easily as the killer had slipped out the back door of my shop.

I straightened. That was it. A place I hadn't checked for clues yet.

"You all right?"

"Yes, I realized I need to do something. Thanks for your help, Nancy," I said as I hurried out the door toward the space behind the shop. Maybe I'd find my next clue.

Back at Whispering Pages, I ignored how the skeleton's empty eye sockets seemed to judge me as I wound between the shelves and opened the back door. A gust of cool air greeted me, and I shivered as I stepped outside into the small parking lot the businesses shared. The faint strains of the high school marching band a few blocks away was carried on the breeze.

Jiji joined me, sniffing at random things near the dumpster in the corner. She sniffed at a cupcake wrapper on the ground, and I couldn't help but glance toward the back of Sugarplum Delights. Nancy had been acting weird when I brought up Nana's missing money, and I was pretty sure it wasn't just in my head.

Could she have something to do with the missing money? If Mr. James had been bothering her too, I'm sure extra money would've been helpful, but I had a hard time imagining her stealing from one of her best friends. Then again, people were capable of all sorts of things—like cheating on you with your college roommate. Maybe Nancy knew something she wasn't saying. Was she trying to throw me off by telling me the cases weren't connected even when they were?

No, I was being silly. If I'd learned anything from my experience with Sebastian, it was that I needed to have more faith in people and be less willing to jump to conclusions without solid evidence. Even I could tell that my opinions kept flipping back and forth, but I couldn't help it.

A door opened behind me with a creak, and I spun around to find Cooper exiting their shop in a pair of blue jeans and a green T-shirt.

"We keep running into each other," he said. "It must be fate, Harp-sicle."

"I'm not a food, Coop." I laughed. Jiji darted away, disappearing between two garbage cans. "And us running into each other might have something to do with the fact that we work literally right next door to one another."

He shrugged and crossed his arms, drumming the fingers of one hand against his other arm. "That also sounds like fate, if you ask me."

"I suppose you could think of it that way, if you wanted to."

"Do you need help with anything?"

"No, I'm okay." I studied him from the corner of my eye. He was acting so casual that I wondered if Sebastian had told him about my accusation. Was he really that chill, or did he not know?

"Is there a reason you're out here poking around the garbage?" He gave me a lopsided smile, then straightened. "I know. You're investigating, aren't you?"

My phone rang, and a glance proved it was an unknown number. "Sorry, I better get this."

He waved as I stepped back into the store and answered, "Hello."

"Hi, is this Miss Coleman?"

"Yes, it is."

"This is Dean Thomas from Whisper Hollow Heritage Bank. I was hoping we could set up an appointment to meet sometime soon."

My stomach tried to tie itself in knots. "About what?"

"About the property you are currently renting on Main Street."

"Of course." I tried not to let my voice shake. "When would you like to meet?"

"If you could come in on the sixteenth at noon, that would work best."

"All right." I swallowed, praying that wouldn't be the moment I'd lose Nana's shop for good. "I'll be there."

Chapter 13

What Does Time Heal Faster: Your Wounds or Your Credit Score?

Between running the store, searching for clues about the killer, and planning the party, the next few days flew by. Suddenly, it was time for my meeting at the bank.

I showed up at noon to find Sebastian and Cooper getting out of a car.

Cooper flashed another megawatt smile. "What did I tell you? Fate."

"And the fact that we live in a small town," I said, though it was getting harder to ignore all the times I'd bumped into Cooper. It might've been Sebastian whom Jiji tried to tie me to with that string, but it was Cooper who kept popping up. And I wasn't sure how I felt about that.

Sebastian gave a curt nod, then turned to his brother. "Come on, Coop. I don't want to be late."

"You coming inside?" Cooper shifted his weight from foot to foot as if even the small delay was too much stillness for him.

"In a minute." I waved them on.

"See ya later, precious," Cooper called as Sebastian dragged him away.

Before they went through the front doors, I heard Sebastian say, "Don't call her that. It makes you sound like Gollum."

"But I've struck out with all the nicknames to do with Harper. I need—"

The door swung shut behind them, cutting off the rest of Cooper's sentence. I couldn't help but smile. First, Sebastian recognized Jiji's name from *Kiki's Delivery Service,* and now a *Lord of the Rings* reference. That proved it. He *was* a nerd.

I pulled out my phone to let Grace know I was heading into the meeting. She sent me back a thumbs up and a phone emoji, telling me to call her after.

Sucking in a breath, I headed inside. A bulletin board standing guard near the front door displayed community announcements, local events, and a few lost-and-found notices. Soft, earthy tones dominated the decor, and the wooden accents gave the space a rustic charm.

"Welcome." An older woman in a button-up shirt and a pair of slacks gave me a broad smile as I entered. Her red hair was pulled into a braid that rested over her shoulder and fell to her waist.

"I have an appointment with Dean Thomas." I checked the note on my phone to verify I had the right name.

"Oh wonderful. You're the last one." She led me across the lobby.

"The last one?"

"Yes, they're all waiting for you."

"They?"

She knocked on a door against the far wall, then opened it without waiting, revealing the interior of a small room where Sebastian, Cooper, and Nancy sat around a sleek wooden table.

My eyes widened. "What are you all doing here?"

A man in a dark suit with black hair cropped close to his head nodded to the table. "If you'll have a seat, Ms. Coleman, I'll explain everything."

I made my way to the open chair, which sat in a puddle of sunlight that streamed through a large window on the far wall. The seat was next to Sebastian, and in my attempts not to look at him, I made eye contact with Cooper, who sat across from me.

He mouthed, *Fate.*

"Now I'm sure you're curious why I've gathered you here today, so I'll get straight to the point." Mr. Thomas cleared his throat and straightened his purple tie before glancing at each of us. "According to the instructions in Mr. James's will, I've been tasked with acting on behalf of the bank, which is the executor and creditor of his estate."

I swallowed and focused on Mr. Thomas instead of the warmth of Sebastian's arm next to mine on the table.

"So what does this all mean?" Nancy folded her hands in her lap. It was weird seeing her without an apron on.

"To put it simply, your landlord owed us a lot of money, and—"

"But he owns so much property on Main Street," I blurted.

Mr. Thomas gave me a look, and I felt like a scolded schoolgirl again.

"Sorry," I muttered. Though I guess that explained why he was hounding all of us. Knowing he was probably as stressed about money as I was didn't make me like him any more, but it made me dislike him a little less.

"We're foreclosing on the building."

"So we'll have to figure out our leases with the new owner?" I asked.

"Unless *we* decide to buy it," Sebastian said.

Mr. Thomas nodded. "You *could* attend the auction and buy the building, as long as you're the highest bidder."

Sebastian and Cooper looked at each other while Nancy and I exchanged glances. For a long moment, none of us said anything. Either we were all too eager and didn't want to seem greedy, or we were all too poor. I knew which one I was.

"How much do you imagine it'll go for?" I laced my fingers together in my lap and squeezed.

"There is another interested buyer, so I assume the bank will try to sell it for five hundred thousand at least, but it's hard to tell for sure with auctions. If you don't have enough to buy it, you might be able to negotiate a contract with the new owner, or they might ask you to vacate the premise." Mr. Thomas's attention flicked to the clock on the wall.

Cooper grimaced and drummed his fingers on the table. "I'd rather we go in on the purchase together."

Nancy nodded so vigorously that some gray hair slipped from her bun. "I'd be interested in that."

"Me too," I agreed, though the thought made me nauseous. Or exhilarated. It was hard to tell which. Even if we split the cost between our three shops, we'd need to raise enough to make sure we were the highest bidder. I bit my lip. I'd probably need to come up with over a hundred and fifty thousand dollars. I'd never had that much money in my life.

"The auction will be at the end of the month, so you have until then to decide what you wish to do," Mr. Thomas said. "I know Mr. James was planning on combining your three shops into one business to pay off his debts—"

"Wait, what?" My mouth fell open. So he hadn't been planning on evicting just *me*. He was going to kick all of us out. No wonder he'd been hounding us to leave. I glanced at the others' faces, but they all seemed surprised. That, or one of them was a really good actor.

"Are you even allowed to tell us that?" Sebastian asked.

He would be a stickler for the rules.

"He's dead, Seb. I don't think it matters much," Cooper muttered.

"Mr. Moore, your brother is correct," Mr. Thomas said. "Confidentiality no longer applies when the client is deceased."

I swallowed past the dryness in my mouth. If any of us had known about Mr. James's plan, it would look like a motive for killing him. But since everyone seemed as shocked by the news as me, I had to think outside the box. Who else had something to gain from his death?

Mr. Thomas gave us a few more details about the auction, then the four of us walked out of the bank and into the parking lot. The dark sky reflected my mood, and gusts of wind tossed my hair around my face.

"So . . . that was sort of intense." Cooper crossed his arms and looked around the group. "Did anyone know Mr. James was planning on evicting us?"

"No," Nancy said in a shaky voice as we stopped by our cars.

"I wonder what he was hoping to do with the building." When I realized I was biting my nails again, I pulled my hand away from my mouth.

"Let's focus on what's important right now." Sebastian glanced at the lightning flashing overhead. "I think it's in our best interests to buy the building so none of us lose our businesses, but can we make it happen?"

Nancy nodded. "I have some money saved for retirement that I could invest, and the rest I'll get from the bank."

"Are you sure that's smart?" Cooper paced around the parking lot.

"I'd rather spend money on this than pay someone else's mortgage every month," she said.

"Coop and I can cover ours since we'll split the amount." Sebastian pointed between him and his brother, and the three turned to look at me.

My stomach dropped faster than my bank account balance. "I don't have it right now, but I'll figure it out." Hopefully.

Thunder rumbled overhead as if disagreeing with me.

Nancy patted my shoulder. "Don't worry, dear. You can get a loan from the bank. You don't need to have all that money right now."

"Thanks, Nancy. I'll look into it." I gave her a feeble smile.

"So we're agreed? The four of us are going to go in on the property?" Sebastian asked.

"Give me a chance to look into a loan first," I said. "We have until the end of the month, so no need to rush it."

"True." Nancy smiled at me, her expression as soft as her famous cupcakes. "Since the bank gave us until Halloween, let's wait and talk to them then."

Sebastian met my gaze, then looked away quickly, reminding me of our awkward conversation.

"Hey, Cooper—Coop," I called, "could I talk to you for a minute?"

"Only if you promise it'll be more than a minute." He winked, even though a minute might be all we had before the storm hit.

While I normally would've had to bite back a smile at his flirting, my head was too full of other things. Like the potential of buying the building with the two guys I had accused of murder. I waited until the others were in their cars, then said, "Did Sebastian say anything to you?"

Cooper ran a hand through his thick hair. "Of course."

My stomach dropped.

"He says things to me all the time," he continued in a conspiratorial whisper. "I know he gives off the whole sexy-and-silent vibe, but don't be fooled. The guy hardly shuts up."

"No, I mean did he say anything about me?"

Cooper's eyes narrowed. "Should he have?"

We stared at each other while I debated what to say. It didn't seem like Cooper knew . . . so did that mean Sebastian had kept my accusation to himself? I couldn't help but glance over at him, and our eyes met through his driver's side window. He looked away, and so did I.

When I turned back to Cooper, he was looking between the two of us. "Did Sebastian ask you out or something?"

"What?" My stomach twisted. How had he come to that conclusion? "No, of course not."

"Then why are you curious if he's said anything about you? Are you interested in him?"

I flushed and willed the heat to leave my face. "Don't be silly." I wasn't, was I?

"So why are we having this conversation?" There went Cooper's eyebrow again. "I'm not totally sure what it is you want to know."

"I sort of . . . embarrassed myself in front of him the other day, and I wasn't sure if he'd said anything to you or not."

"Because you care what I think?" He smirked at me.

I threw my hands in the air. "You're impossible."

"But you didn't say I was wrong."

"Fine, yeah. In this case, I guess I do care." At least I cared enough to not want him to know that I'd suspected them of murder, even if I was still trying to look into their alibis.

"Come on, Coop!" Sebastian yelled out the open driver's side window.

"I better go," he said. "But I'm so glad we had this strange chat."

I opened my car door and slid inside, then leaned back against the headrest and took a few deep breaths as the other cars pulled out around me. Honestly, I shouldn't care so much what either of the brothers thought, and I definitely shouldn't have bothered trying to clear the air. I'd only made things more awkward for myself. But now I was free to worry about how I was supposed to afford the building.

Large raindrops splattered against my windshield, blurring the world around me and making it hard to see clearly—sort of like the murder. Instead of driving back in the deluge, I stared at Grace's picture on my phone screen for a long moment before hitting the *call* button. Was it a good idea? I'd kept the truth from her this long . . .

I drummed my fingers along the steering wheel while I waited for her to pick up.

"What's up, Harp?"

"I met with someone at the bank today, and they offered me, Nancy, and the Moore brothers a chance to buy our building." My stomach tightened with nerves, and I clutched the wheel.

"That's amazing," she squealed over the phone. "Not having to rent it anymore would be a huge step up for your business."

"Yeah, but the problem is, I don't have a hundred grand or more lying around."

She laughed. "Most people don't. That's what loans are for," she said. "And the nice thing is, I bet you could have the loan paid off in ten years or so with some aggressive payments."

This was it. The part I'd been dreading. "Yeah, but I'm not sure if the bank will approve me for a loan."

"Don't be silly," she said. "Why wouldn't they approve you?"

I swallowed past the dryness in my throat. This was another reason I'd run away to Whisper Hollow—an embarrassing secret I'd kept even from Grace. "Because Tate ruined my credit score."

Chapter 14

Papers and Hips Don't Lie

"How did he ruin your credit score?" Grace screeched into my ear.

"Remember that new car he bought?" I pulled out of the parking lot. "Well, he couldn't afford it unless someone cosigned with him."

"Tell me you didn't."

I shrugged. "I thought it would be okay since we were engaged, but then he kept being late with the payments—"

"So it wasn't enough for him to break your heart, he had to break your credit score too?" She swore again. "This is unbelievable. If I ever see that lying cheater again, I'm gonna wring his skinny little neck."

"Anyway, the point is, I don't think I'll get approved for that much." I switched lanes and headed toward Main Street. "I could maybe get half of it, but even then, where am I supposed to come up with the rest?"

Grace sighed, and I pictured her pinching the bridge of her nose.

"How long do you have?" she asked.

"The auction is at the end of the month." If we bought the building outright, I wouldn't have to pay a mortgage, so I could potentially use the money set aside for my next rent payment, but that wouldn't make a dent in what I'd need. If only I could find Nana's missing money somehow, but it was probably long gone.

"Hmm . . . I'm not sure. That isn't a lot of time, but I'll keep thinking about it." Something crashed in the background, and she swore. "I gotta go. Kelsey dropped a cup and there's glass all over the floor."

"Okay."

"Chin up, Harp. We'll figure this out," she said before the line went dead.

A few minutes later, I was back at the shop and reopening Whispering Pages. A few hours and a few customers later, María bustled into the shop with a paper in her hand. She shook her umbrella off outside the door, then walked over. She tried to pet Jiji, who jumped onto the top of a nearby shelf and looked at her for a second before licking her own leg.

"Someday, I'll get her to like me," she muttered before putting a mockup flier on the counter in front of me. "What do you think of this?"

The flier had a border of pointed black hats and grinning jack-o'-lanterns with black and purple font announcing the details of a Halloween party on Friday the twenty-eighth at Whispering Pages. Two days before the next meeting with the bank.

"It looks great."

Could the party be my chance to earn some extra money? The thought of earning everything I needed in one night was ridiculous, but more people meant more sales, so it was worth a shot.

"I know you were on the fence about if we should do it, but—"

"Let's do it." I smiled at her. "You're right. This could be exactly the sort of marketing I need to get people in the store."

María's eyebrows flew into her hairline. "I didn't realize I was so persuasive."

"Yeah, you and the fact that I need to start earning some money if I don't want to say goodbye to my grandmother's shop." I looked around, taking in the rows of shelves I'd wandered among as a child.

"Paying for this party is a good thing," María said. "Money spent today might change the fate of nations tomorrow."

"C. S. Lewis?"

She shook her head. "Robert Jordan. Nice try though."

"Okay, so what should I do?" I glanced at the paper again.

"I'll take care of the publicity, and you figure out refreshments and music. The decorations are already done." She looked around the shop with an appreciative grin.

"I had an idea for the food already," I said. "What if we work with Nancy next door? She makes the cutest cupcakes, and I'm sure she'd appreciate the extra business too." I had my suspicions about her, but I couldn't let that stand in the way of getting the best food in town.

"Sounds great. Why don't you order a hundred." María grabbed the paper and put it in her bag. "I'm going to make a bunch of copies of these and put them all around town. I'll also create an event page online so you can maximize your social media. It's going to be great."

"A hundred?" I looked around, imagining a hundred people crammed into the shop.

As if reading my mind, María laughed. "Not everyone will come at the same time. People will probably trickle in and out throughout the night. But I want to make sure we have enough refreshments. I'll pick up some smaller things to go with the cupcakes."

"Are you sure?" I asked. "This seems like a lot of work for you."

She tucked a strand of hair behind her ear. "That's okay. I love planning parties. You're practically doing me a favor."

I laughed. "Right. I'm sure."

The door opened, and Jiji jumped onto the counter in front of me. Not at all bothered by his rain-kissed hair, Cooper snagged a candy from the cauldron as he walked by and patted the skeleton on the head. "What are you ladies up to?"

"I'm helping Harper plan a Halloween party she's hosting at the bookshop," María said.

"Sounds fun."

"I better go. I've got so much to do. I can't wait." María headed toward the door, but once she was behind Cooper's back, she looked at me and winked.

I flushed and busied myself rearranging the display table of Halloween books near the front. "What's up, Coop?"

"I wanted to talk to you about the meeting today." He popped the candy into his mouth, then took a step closer. "You seemed a little off in the parking lot."

Jiji gave him one offended look—who knew why—then jumped off the counter, her tail held high as she strutted away.

While it was sweet he'd stopped by, I didn't want to admit my financial problems to him, especially when I still clung to the faint hope of finding Nana's money and it miraculously solving my problems. "Thanks for checking on me."

He put one hand on my arm. "You don't need to stress about this."

I smiled at him. "I'm okay."

"You like to stay busy, huh? Opening a business, throwing parties, tracking down murder suspects."

"It's better than giving my mind time to wander."

Cooper leaned a little closer, and I froze. He had a habit of breaking the touch barrier when I least expected it. His breath smelled like the caramel apple candy he was sucking on.

It had been a while since I was so close to anyone—a while since Tate—and it felt nice. I'd missed having someone who worried about me or took care of me. Just because I didn't need it, didn't mean I didn't want it.

"You don't need to worry," he said. "Even if you can't pay your portion, Seb and I talked, and we'd be willing to get a loan to cover your portion and let you keep renting from us. Nothing would have to change."

"Wow. That's really nice of you." But it didn't stop the tension in my stomach from fizzling out like an old soda. While he'd intended to be thoughtful, it sounded like someone else telling me they didn't think I'd succeed. I wanted to own my business and pay my own mortgage, not be stuck paying someone else rent again. And while *I* was allowed a little self-doubt, I didn't want to hear doubt from others.

"Thanks. I'll keep that in mind," I said.

He turned toward the door. "Well, I better get back to work before Seb tracks me down."

"Sounds rough," I said, shooting for the lighthearted tone from earlier.

He pushed the door open. "The roughest."

Once the rain had slowed to a drizzle, I made my way to Sugarplum Delights, where half the tables were full.

"First Cooper and now you." Nancy smiled as I reached the counter. "Was seeing me at the bank not enough?"

I laughed and tried not to think about how I suspected this woman—who I'd known since I was a child—of murder. "It's never enough, but also, María and I have decided to go ahead with hosting that party, and I wanted to order some of your cupcakes."

"Oh, perfect." Nancy's eyes lit up, and she smiled so wide that the crow's feet at the corner of her eyes deepened. "What a fun way to celebrate our big news about the building too."

"Yeah," I said, trying to match her enthusiasm.

"Let me grab a bulk order form, and I'll—"

"Can we get some help?" a mom with two little girls called out.

Nancy and I looked over to find the tablecloth soaked and a puddle of liquid on the floor.

"I need to invest in better lids for the kids' drinks," Nancy muttered.

"That's okay. I can clean up while you help them," I said.

Nancy grabbed some rags from a counter along the back wall, then gestured to a door next to the kitchen ones. "I've got it. Pop back into my office and grab a form off my desk. You'll recognize it because it'll say *Bulk Orders* across the top."

"All right." I walked into her office and went straight to her desk. Without trying to mess things up, I shifted around Post-it notes, a giant calendar, and some bills before finding a stack of papers under a book. I moved a sheet with different menu items written on it, and another that looked like a supply order form, then I found it. I lifted the bulk order form from a stack on her desk, and my gaze snagged on a paper partially hidden underneath.

It had the same slanted writing as the note I'd found on my door almost two weeks ago—the note from Mr. James. The top was ripped, taking the salutation and the first few words with it, but I could read the rest.

—writing to inform you that, due to circumstances beyond my control, I will be terminating your lease agreement effective December 31st. While you have been a good tenant, my vision for this property has taken

*a different turn, and I'm planning on combining this shop with some
others to create a new store.*

I skimmed over the rest of the letter, then read it a second time,
my chest growing tight. The letter was proof that Nancy had known
about Mr. James's intention to displace us from our stores.

Another crack of thunder rumbled the building.

Was Nancy the person I should've suspected all along? If I searched
her desk, would I find the key she'd so mysteriously *misplaced?* She
lived alone, so it would've been easy for her to slip away and get to Mr.
James, and knowing her, she'd probably read my letter from Nana and
discovered where the money was.

The door opened, and Nancy bustled in. "Did you find it?"

Boy did I ever.

"Yeah, I think so." I forced a trembling smile and tried not to look
at the paper on her desk.

Nancy walked over and wiped her hands on her apron.

"Is this it?" I stepped in front of the desk and held the bulk form
out while swiping the other paper behind my back. If I needed more
evidence, the letter to Nancy would be a good start.

Nancy skimmed the form and bobbed her head. "That's the one.
Let's fill it out together, and I can make sure I have all the supplies I
need for the order."

"Can I take it with me and check with María first to get a better idea
of how many people she's thinking?"

She looked at me for a long moment. Could she hear how loudly
my heart was pounding?

Nancy handed the form back. "As long as you get it to me at least a
week before the party, it should be fine."

"Perfect. I can do that." As soon as Nancy turned for the door, I
folded the form and letter together and shoved them into my pocket.

Hopefully, Nancy didn't have a camera in her office. "I'll figure it out as soon as I can."

"Can't wait," Nancy said as we re-entered the bustling bakery.

Rain pounded against the windows, distorting the outside world into blurred shapes. It felt like I was in some sort of twilight zone where my grandmother's best friend might be capable of murder and theft.

I looked around at the crowds, trying to act normal. "Well, you seem pretty busy now, and I'd better get back to the shop."

"Are you sure you want to leave? It's raining cats and dogs again out there."

"I'm sure."

"All right, then. See you soon, dear." Nancy waved and bustled to the counter to greet a couple who was shaking off their umbrella by the door.

I hurried outside and sucked in a breath of bracing air as soon as the door closed behind me. What in the actual heck was going on? Without stopping, I ran the few feet to Whispering Pages. As I fumbled for my key, the icy rain pelted my skin and soaked my hair. Re-entering the shop, I closed the door behind me and shivered.

With a sigh, I popped in my AirPod and called Grace again.

After a few rings, she picked up. "Two calls in one day. How unusual."

"I know, but I need to talk to someone, and it needs to be someone who doesn't live here and know these people."

"Why? What happened?" Her tone sharpened with concern.

I used a towel from my office to dry off. "The problem is, I found a letter from Mr. James on Nancy's desk, telling her he was going to evict her and change her shop."

Grace gasped. "So she knew the whole time?"

"She knew, and she lied." I pulled the paper out of my pocket again. At least it hadn't gotten wet. It smelled like a mix of pumpkin and something strange—a scent I couldn't quite put my finger on.

After a pause, Grace said, "Are you suggesting Nancy could be the killer?" It was as hard for her to imagine as it was for me, considering Nancy had been around through all our childhood visits.

"I don't know." I bit my thumbnail. "But I'm not the only one that thinks that's weird, right?"

"Yeah, it does seem odd," Grace agreed. "It's hard to picture Nosy Nancy doing that."

"I know." I sighed and paced around the shop. "But it wouldn't be weird for her to know about the money Nana left me. She's the one who gave me the letter. She could've read it first."

"In a twisted way, it sort of makes sense," Grace said. "According to the crime shows and murder mystery novels, it isn't unusual for the criminal to insert themselves into an investigation and want to be a part of it, and Nosy Nancy has been there every step of the way."

"Do you think that's why she's been helping me?"

Grace snorted. "I guess you could call it helping. She's been giving you clues to everyone but herself and sending you on a series of wild-goose chases."

"But she did mention the key to me at least," I said. "Do you think she would've done that if it was her?"

"I don't know. She could be innocent, or that could also have been to throw you off her trail." Grace paused, then asked, "So are you going to confront her like you did Sebastian?"

"Of course not. That was a total disaster."

"Then are you going to turn her in?"

"Not without more evidence." I sank into my favorite chair again, and Jiji hopped onto my lap, curled into a ball, and started purring.

At least one of us was happy.

"Okay, let's think this through," Grace said. "If Nancy did it, she would've needed motive, means, and opportunity."

"We know she had motive because she was the only one who knew about Mr. James's plans to evict us."

"That's a mark against her."

I climbed back to my feet to pace again, making Jiji jump off with a disgruntled yowl. "And if that key wasn't *missing* like she said, she could've gotten into the shop and lured Mr. James inside."

"Strike two."

"What I don't understand is what she was doing in my shop in the first place?"

"Maybe she was there for Nana's money, and Mr. James caught her in the act?"

"Maybe." I stopped pacing as something else came back to me. "Nancy's shop was closed the morning I discovered the body. I remember thinking how odd it was."

Grace made a thoughtful noise. "That is odd," she said. "What was the murder weapon again?"

"A hammer with a blue handle." I shuddered as I glanced at Jiji, who settled into my vacated spot and closed her eyes again. She was the one who'd found it under a bookshelf, one end covered with dried blood and who knows what else.

Something rustled on Grace's end, then she said, "She probably had it lying around."

For a long moment, the only noise was the rain pounding on the roof, then Grace said, "I dunno, Harp. It doesn't look too good for Nancy."

"I know, but it didn't look too good for me when he was discovered in *my* shop. I feel like I owe it to Nancy for all the help she's given me since I moved here to not confront her with my suspicions. Not to mention that she's one of Nana's oldest friends."

"Maybe you shouldn't confront her after all. Take what you know to the police and let them handle it," Grace said. "I don't want you facing down a killer."

I shuddered. "Good point. Okay, I'll keep my eyes peeled for any more clues, and if the police don't make much progress on the case, I'll talk to them in a few days."

"Sounds like a plan." Grace said something muffled to one of her children, then to me, she said, "Did you check to see if Nancy was a customer at Blossom Boutique in the last two weeks?"

"Not yet, but I'll do it now." I pulled my phone from my pocket and thumbed through the photos until I got to the ones from that day. Zooming in a bit, I skimmed through the names.

"It's there," I whispered as I stopped on the second page that said *Nancy Simmon*.

"Harp?"

"Yeah?"

"Be careful," she said. "I'd rather not be an only child."

"Thanks for the vote of confidence." I hung up and tried to figure out my next move now that I knew Nancy had had motive to kill Mr. James and she'd lied.

Chapter 15

To Date or Not to Date

Balancing on top of the ladder, I tied one end of the banner advertising next week's Halloween party above the front door of Whispering Pages while María held it steady. I couldn't help but glance over at Nancy's shop. It had been almost a week since my discovery of the paper in her office, and while I hadn't found anything else to take to the police, I also hadn't found anything to make me think she was innocent.

"Hello? Are you listening?" María asked.

"I'm sorry. What?" I glanced at her as I climbed down the ladder.

She laughed and shook her head, making the afternoon sunlight glint off dark braid. "I said, can you believe the party is only a week away?"

"No, I can't." I stepped back to study the banner and make sure it was hanging straight. "Time is flying."

A week until the party. A week until the money was due to buy the building. A week until I had to decide to either confront Nancy or take the information to the police because I couldn't very well buy the building alongside a potential killer. It was all coming too fast.

"I think I've got everything ready. I've put up fliers all over town. Recruited a few volunteers to set up games on the shop's second floor, and I asked my mother to make these super gross severed witch finger cookies and other treats. It's going to be awesome."

"Sounds great."

"And you ordered the cupcakes from Nancy already, right?"

I tore my gaze from Sugarplum Delights, where it had drifted once more. "Not quite."

Her eyes widened. "Why not? The party's only a week away. I thought you picked up the form last week."

"I'm sorry. I did go last week, but then I got . . . distracted." I didn't have a real excuse to give her since I couldn't tell her it was my doubts keeping me away.

The wrinkle between her eyes disappeared as a grin brightened her face. "Distracted, huh? It wouldn't have anything to do with a tall, dark, and handsome man who happens to work next door and keeps flirting with you, now would it?"

I flushed. "Of course not." But I still couldn't tell her I hadn't ordered the food because I'd been too busy trying to decide whether Nancy was a murderer or not.

"Riiiight." With a smirk, María looked at the checklist she'd pulled from her pocket. "Because it's definitely a coincidence that the day you were supposed to place the order was the same day he came over to 'check on' you."

"Yes, it *is* a coincidence."

She wiggled her eyebrows and helped me take the ladder down. "Are you sure? Because you two were looking awfully cozy when I peeked through the window."

"You looked through the window?" I wasn't sure if I wanted to laugh or scold her. "I'm serious, María. Nothing happened. He came to talk about our meeting with Mr. Thomas."

The day after the meeting, I'd filled her in on what the bank had said about the auction, and her enthusiasm for the party had doubled.

"Really? Because, from where I stood, if you two had been standing any closer, you could've shared the same shirt. Or maybe the point was to not be wearing any shirts at all," she added with a wink.

"María!"

Her smile widened as we carried the ladder through the shop to the storage room. The chorus of "Thriller" drifted to us from the speaker I'd set up at the desk. After two weeks of Nana's record, I'd gotten tired of the same eerie music.

"Never mind. It doesn't even matter," I said, ducking under a hanging spiderweb. "Nothing happened, and nothing is going to happen."

"I think he likes you."

"Yes, but like you've said, he seems to like most women in town." Plus, being around the brothers left my feelings in a tangled snarl. Sebastian was too much of an enigma to get a read on, and Cooper was too friendly and too similar to Tate for me to fully trust.

María muttered something in Spanish that made me wish I'd paid more attention in Señora Garcia's class, then shrugged. "Well, if you won't get that order placed. I guess I'll have to."

I opened my mouth, then closed it. What could I say to stop her without sounding like a paranoid idiot? Instead, I said, "Thanks for all your help, María. It means a lot."

She smiled, the expression lighting up her whole face. "You're giving me a chance to flex my party-planning muscles." And with that, she marched out the door and turned left toward Sugarplum Delights.

I spent the next hour helping a few customers and figuring out how to work the smoke machine—which María borrowed from someone in town since she thought it would be fun to have—while Jiji constantly meowed at me and demanded attention. The jingle of the front door made me look up from where I stood by the checkout counter.

"Hey, neighbor." Cooper flashed a smile at me as he walked in. For a moment, the afternoon light framed him in gold, highlighting the subtle undertones in his hair and making him a dark shape at the entrance. Then he took another step, revealing a pair of blue jeans and a white T-shirt under the V of his cream sweater.

"What, no nickname today?"

"*Neighbor* wasn't enough for you?"

I laughed. "What can I do for you?"

"*That* is a great question." He sauntered forward, leaned against the counter with one elbow, and looked at the smoke machine. "But first, it looks like I should see what I can do for you. You seem to be struggling with that."

I laughed and pushed a loose strand of hair behind my ear. "Is it that obvious?"

"Sort of. Yeah. Totally."

"I'm not the best with technology, and I can't get the piece of crap to work," I said. "Let me guess. Is this one of your talents?"

"Well, I'm not as good as Seb, but I'm guessing I can help. Let me see." Cooper leaned in so both of our heads were bent over the machine.

Cooper was handsome. I couldn't deny that. His hair hung to his ears in slight waves, emphasizing his strong jaw, which was similar to Sebastian's.

Jiji meowed, and I reached out to pet her while Cooper worked on the machine.

"Is that the same cat that allegedly ruined your sweater?" His expression was serious, but his eyes twinkled, betraying his teasing.

"There's no *allegedly* about it." I folded my arms across my chest. "You saw my sweater that day. I was lucky I caught her when I did, or I would've been walking around half naked!"

"Lucky indeed," he murmured.

I elbowed him in the side. "Shut up."

He pulled back a few seconds later and shot me a victorious smile as smoke started billowing from the hole in the front of the machine.

"Thank you!" I dropped my gaze to the smoke machine, hoping he hadn't caught me staring, although I couldn't resist glancing at him again. "How did you do that?"

He winked. "I can't tell you all my secrets, now can I?"

"I suppose not." I laughed. "But you can tell me what I can do to thank you."

He leaned back and studied me, then reached into the chest pocket of his T-shirt. "You can go on a date with me." He pulled his hand from his pocket and held out a miniature glass rose.

"Oh, I . . ." I bit my lip and looked at the flower, then up at his hopeful face. I couldn't deny that I was attracted to Cooper, but I wasn't sure I should go out with him. I wasn't sure I was ready to go out with anyone.

His smile turned lopsided, and he lowered the flower but still held it out. "Not exactly the response I was hoping for."

"I'm sorry."

"No, it's okay. You don't have to apologize. You already warned me you're against dating—"

"That wasn't what I said—"

"And that if I wanted to date you, I'd have to work my butt off—"

"That *definitely* wasn't what I said."

He smiled at me, his dimple peeking out. "Okay, you might not have said that last part in so many words. But it's clearly what you meant."

I laughed. "I can't tell if your confidence is inspiring or troubling."

"Funny." He raised one eyebrow. "Seb always says it's both."

"Well, anyway, I don't know if it's a good idea. I'm—"

"It's okay, Harper. You don't have to soften it for me." He held the flower out again. "And you can still have this. I made it for you."

"Oh, thanks." I accepted the glass rose, which was smooth and slightly warm from his skin. "That was thoughtful of you."

He leaned close, so our eyes were level. "I'm giving up today, but that doesn't mean I'm giving up on you. You might've won this battle, but as they say, 'love is a battlefield,' and the war is far from over."

With that, Cooper turned around and strolled away from the shop, leaving me staring after him.

I couldn't date Cooper. Despite his gorgeous smile, friendly attitude, and the way he'd checked in on me—in fact, he'd been good about checking in with me almost since day one—I still wasn't ready to date anyone. Not that I needed to worry about that. According to María, Cooper didn't date. Not seriously, anyway. And while Cooper was smooth and often seemed to know the right thing to say, unlike his perplexing brother, he still reminded me too much of Tate.

Even still, once the door closed behind him, I glanced around to confirm that the shop was empty, then called Grace—no need to talk about my love life, or lack thereof, in front of anyone from town.

"What's up, sis?"

"Cooper asked me out," I said by way of greeting.

"He did?" she squealed. "That's amazing!"

I paced around the store, straightening book spines and shelving a few books that had been left out. "No, it isn't. Because I said no."

"Why did you do that?"

"You know why."

She sighed. "Harp, it's been eight months since Tate the Lying Cheater. Don't you think it's time to move on?"

"Obviously not, or I wouldn't have turned down Cooper." I pushed a book back into place with a little too much force.

"Okay, listen. I get that he broke your heart and you need time, but by not going on dates with anyone else, you're letting him continue to have power over you."

I opened my mouth to say something, but she rushed on almost as if she could see me and knew I was going to argue.

"And I'm not saying you need to jump right back into the dating pool and find a new boyfriend or anything, but I don't think it would hurt for you to put yourself out there. A date doesn't mean you have to commit to anyone. Dip your toes in and test out the water instead of spending your Friday nights rereading Brandon Sanderson books."

"Hey, I'll have you know, they're amazing."

"Yes, but a book isn't going to keep you company."

"That's not exactly true."

I could almost hear her rolling her eyes. "Fine. A book isn't going to keep you warm in bed."

"That's what Jiji is for." My cheeks warmed. "Besides, you said I didn't need to look for a relationship right now."

"And you don't," she said. "But going on dates would at least mean you're taking small steps in the right direction if you want to find someone—and I know you do. You've read *Pride and Prejudice* too many times for me to believe otherwise."

"Okay, fine. Maybe I'll say *yes* the next time someone asks me on a date." Cooper had said he was going to try again. The thought made my stomach flutter.

"Or you could go next door and let him know that you've changed your mind."

I grabbed the long-handled duster from under the counter and started wiping the spines of the books on shelves. I might as well put my pacing to good use, after all. "I can't do that."

"Sure you can. Go over and say, 'Hey, sorry about earlier, but I would like to go out. When are you free?'"

"I think I'd rather wait." And avoid the chance of running into Sebastian again.

"Come on, Harp," she pled through the phone. "Take a chance and put yourself out there again. Prove to yourself that Tate the Lying Cheater doesn't have power over you anymore and you're moving on."

I glance at my bare ring finger, but for the first time in a while, my heart no longer ached when I looked at it. Yes, discovering that he cheated on me still sucked. Yes, I'd driven to Grace's house a sobbing mess. Back then, his betrayal had felt like the end of the world, but there was more to my life than Tate now. Even his random text messages over the last few weeks hadn't affected me as much as they could have.

"You're right."

"I am?"

"Why are you acting surprised now, after pushing this on me?"

"I'm not surprised about being right," she said. "I'm surprised about you admitting it."

I laughed. "There's the Grace I know and love."

"Okay, I'm hanging up now so you can go over there right now and talk to Cooper."

"Right now?"

"Right now." She emphasized her words with a click before the line went dead.

I sucked in a deep breath and ran my hands down my pants. I was done letting Tate hold me back, and this date with Cooper, whether it meant anything or not, would be my first step in moving on.

Although I was only going next door, I carefully locked up Whispering Pages. I'd learned my lesson, and I wouldn't let anyone else be killed in my shop.

When I turned around, I bumped into someone carrying a large cake in a box.

"Oh, sorry." I held out a hand to steady them and stepped back.

"Is that you, Harper?" Nancy shifted the box slightly, revealing rosy cheeks.

"Oh, hey Nancy." My stomach clenched. How was I supposed to be normal around her, knowing what I knew?

"Could you give me a hand? I'd hate to drop anything."

"Oh, okay." I accepted the cake from the top of her load, leaving her with two boxes of cupcakes. "You going to the shop?"

"Yup." She walked the last few feet to Sugarplum Delights. "How are the preparations for the party coming along?"

I opened the door with my back, holding it open for her. "I think everything is about ready to go."

"That's great. María swung by earlier and gave me that form. I'll get started on the cupcake order soon."

"Perfect." I forced a smile. "Thanks."

"And are you still feeling okay about the auction? I'll admit, I've been a bundle of nerves since our meeting last week, but I'm trying to stay optimistic." She sighed as she put the cake down on the counter, then looked wistfully around the shop as she tucked a strand of silver hair behind one ear. It glistened like spun sugar in the bakery's warm light. "It's hard to believe this will all finally be mine."

Was it hard to believe, or had she planned it that way? If only I knew whether that money she had saved up for her shop was hers or money she'd stolen from Nana.

"I better get going." I put the cake down and edged toward the door.

"Oh, wait."

I stopped, heart pounding. "Yeah?"

"Did you finally buy some groceries? I haven't seen you in here for the last week or so, and I wanted to make sure you're eating okay."

I studied the gentle lines of her wrinkled face. Was she an excellent actor, or was she genuinely concerned for me and pretending about the news? Or maybe she'd lied about Mr. James but hadn't killed him.

"Yeah, sorry. I thought it was finally time I started saving money."

"Well, that's probably a good idea, but know that I miss you and that you're welcome to pop in any time." She walked behind the counter and slipped on one of her well-worn aprons dusted with flour.

"Nancy"—I hesitated, then decided to go for it—"you'd tell me the truth if I asked, right?"

She smiled, making the wrinkles in her cheeks fold even more. "Of course."

I couldn't help but see the woman who'd given me treats and told me stories when I was little, and my heart twinged. "Are you hiding anything from me?"

Something flickered in her expression, too quickly to track. "No."

Disappointment settled in my stomach like a stone. "Really?"

"Well," she said, biting her lip, "I do have one thing to talk to you about, but I promised Bettye I'd wait."

I blinked at her. Where had that come from? Was she trying to throw me off? Had she talked to Nana about her plans?

"Okay, I'd better go then." I hurried out the door, phone buzzing in my pocket. I fished it out and froze.

What could Tate possibly want to talk about? We had nothing to say to each other, and we hadn't since the night I'd found him with my college roommate. In bed.

With a sharp exhale, I shoved away the memory of their apologies, the way they'd insisted it was a drunken accident. I declined the call. Grace was right. I didn't need anyone else in my life right now, but I did need to get over Tate and stop letting him affect me. And maybe the first step for that would be to start going on dates again. Plus, if I spent some more time with Cooper, maybe I could get more info on his and Sebastian's alibis for the night of the festival.

But first, I did what I should have done a long time ago and blocked Tate's number, then deleted it. He couldn't bother me anymore. Pressing the delete button lifted a weight from my chest, and I continued to Grain and Glass with a smile. Though I could only see Cooper's cream sweater and the back of his dark head crouched down behind the counter, I didn't give myself time to second guess myself.

"I'm sorry about what I said," I said it all in a rush, trying to get it out before he turned around and I'd have to say it to his face.

Cooper stiffened, his shoulders tensing. Despite his bravado, I must've hurt him more than I'd realized.

"I've been sort of hesitant about dating because of what happened with my ex," I continued, "but I would like to go on a date with you." The silence between us lasted a beat too long, and my pounding heart struggled to fill the budding silence. "So, what do you say?"

"I'm sorry."

I took a step back, trying to maintain my smile. I shouldn't have stopped by Grains and Glass after all. But then the voice registered. Wait a minute, that wasn't Cooper, it was—

Sebastian turned around and gave me an inscrutable look. "I don't think that's a good idea."

Chapter 16

Maize Maze

"I'm so sorry!" I backed away from the counter and from Sebastian's curious stare.

Could I be any more of an idiot? How had I asked the wrong brother out? I should've realized it was Sebastian. His hair was shorter than Cooper's. But why was he wearing the same sweater? "I thought you were your brother."

"So you want to go on a date with Cooper?" Sebastian asked in a tone I couldn't quite identify. But considering he'd turned me down, it definitely wasn't jealousy.

"Well, I mean, he asked me out earlier, and I turned him down, so I wanted to let him know I'd changed my mind."

"Why?" He folded his arms across his broad chest.

"Does it matter?" This must be what Cooper meant when he said Sebastian was overprotective.

"I'm making sure you won't hurt Coop, considering how you can't seem to even tell us apart."

My flush deepened. "That's not fair. You're wearing his sweater." I immediately wanted to reel the words back in as soon as they'd slipped out.

Sebastian raised one eyebrow and studied me as if waiting for my explanation. "Yes, well, I spilled something on my shirt."

"Fine." I sighed. "I didn't think I was ready to date again, but I decided it would be a good idea to stop holding onto . . . things from my past and move on. And since Coop asked and he's nice to talk to, I figured he would be a good choice."

His expression softened so subtly I might've missed it had I not been staring at him so intently.

Wait a minute. I wasn't supposed to be staring at Sebastian. I dropped my gaze to his mouth instead of his blue eyes. "Do I have your permission to go out with him?" My sarcasm slipped out again.

A smile ghosted across his face. "I suppose it's fine this time. But his curfew is ten."

I laughed, then froze. Were Sebastian and I flirting while we talked about my date with his brother? While a date was obviously far from any type of commitment—thankfully—flirting with the date's older brother was a little weird. There was just something about Sebastian that either left us fighting or made him impossible to look away from.

The door opened behind me, and I spun around.

"Harper?" Cooper came in with a crate in his arms. "You missed me already?"

"Something like that." I smiled at him, trying to ignore the weight of Sebastian's gaze on me. "I, um, changed my mind about earlier."

"About what specifically?" he asked, eyes dancing.

Oh my, he was going to make me work for it. "About going on a date."

Behind me, the back door closed with a thud, announcing Sebastian's departure.

"What was it that convinced you to accept my invite," Cooper said, "my irresistible charm, my dashing good looks, or my—"

"It was your humility, obviously."

"Naturally. That's one of my best traits." He put the crate on the floor and walked over. "But seriously, what changed?"

"To put it simply, my sister told me to put myself out there again."

Cooper grinned. "Perfect. Tell her I'll pay her later."

I laughed at the thought of him and Grace working together, even though I wouldn't put it past either of them. "So did you want to do something tonight?"

"I have something tonight, though I would much rather spend time with you. I have a bad habit of leaving some things to the last minute." He sighed and shook his head. "Anyway, how about tomorrow evening?"

"Sounds perfect. What would you like to do?"

He grinned in a way that made his dimple come out—he and Sebastian had the same dimple, but in different cheeks. "How do you feel about surprises?"

My thoughts flashed to the moment I'd discovered Tate and Ashley in bed. I pushed down the nausea in my stomach. "Um . . . they aren't my favorite."

"Don't worry. This will be a good one." He put a hand over mine, and I let the warmth from his touch pull me from my memories and back to the present. "I'll swing by around six tomorrow and pick you up."

"Sounds good."

I went back to Whispering Pages and spent the rest of that afternoon and the next day working with María on party prep and catering to a few customers. Kyle was off for the day, so I had to take care of everything myself. Between checking the inventory, cleaning, dealing with customers, working on displays, marketing, and the million other things I had to stay on top of, the day flew by. At least being busy kept me from worrying about the missing money, the unsolved murder, and my looming financial obligation.

At six p.m. sharp the next evening, Cooper knocked on the front door of Whispering Pages before coming in and giving his usual bow. As he straightened, his silly grin slid from his face. "Wow, you look beautiful."

My cheeks heated—stupid blushing cheeks. "Thank you." Considering all I'd done was throw on a bit more makeup and a nicer pair of jeans with an emerald sweater that made my eyes pop, I wasn't sure whether that meant I'd cleaned up or that I needed to wear more makeup on a regular basis. Maybe I normally looked like a mess. "So what are we doing?"

He wagged a finger at me and held the door open. "Nice try, but I said this was going to be a surprise."

I fumbled in my purse for the key to lock up the shop, but no matter how many times I dug through the tissues and papers and gum packets, the key didn't appear. "I can't find my key."

"Did you put it down somewhere this morning—after you got in?"

I closed my eyes and tried to retrace my steps. I'd been a bit distracted since another delivery of books had arrived at almost the same time as me—María had insisted I stock up on more books with a fall feel to capitalize on the crowd coming for the party.

Cooper followed me back inside while I tried to retrace my steps.

"You could use the spare key from this drawer," he said, pulling out a key at the same time I said, "I found it under this stack of papers!"

"Oh, that doesn't work anymore," I said. "I got the locks changed." But as I looked at the spare key, then at him, my stomach twisted uncomfortably. Why was he so familiar with its location? No, I was being paranoid again. I'd already learned that Cooper and Sebastian knew where Nana's spare key was. It wasn't new information. And it didn't really matter since Nancy was the one who'd mysteriously misplaced her key to my shop and lied about the situation with Mr. James.

Cooper dropped the key back into the drawer, and I locked the front door on our way out.

Cooper offered his arm like we were in some sort of romance novel. I laughed and slid my arm through his. The scent of cinnamon and spice wafted from Sugarplum Delights as we walked down the street to the square. A streetlight behind us cast our elongated shadows ahead of us on the sidewalk and made the occasional scarecrows along the path seem weirdly ominous. I shivered and stepped closer to Cooper. Small candles floated on the gurgling fountain in the middle of the town square. Their soft glow reflected off the rippling water.

Cooper led me to a food truck and bought us each a caramel apple.

"Seriously, Cooper, where are we going?" I asked as we climbed into his car with the snacks in hand.

"That is for me to know, and for you to find out."

Cooper drove through town, leaving the city lights behind. About twenty minutes later, he pulled into a parking lot by a field of towering cornstalks. We were far enough from the city that we could see a blanket of stars twinkling overhead and a silvery gleam cast over the field by the moon.

My eyes widened as I took in the bustling parking lot and stalks of corn in the distance. "Is this what I think it is?"

"Only if you're thinking it's a corn maze," Cooper said before quickly adding, "Is that all right? I get it if you aren't comfortable going through with me. I know we haven't known each other very long."

"Are you kidding? I love these!"

His smile turned complacent—sort of like the look Jiji gave after she knocked something off the kitchen table. "I hoped you might."

"Plus, I've got my pepper spray if you try anything." I smiled at him, though my stomach dropped as I remembered spraying Sebastian in the forest. If he were here, he'd never try anything.

We got out of the car, and Cooper paid for our entry, then reclaimed my hand.

"Don't you think it's weird they don't call it a maize maze?" Cooper asked. "It feels like a missed opportunity."

"I guess. I never thought about it before now." I laughed. "But even if it's not called that, thanks for bringing me."

"So you agree it was a good surprise, then?"

"*This* time it was a good surprise," I admitted as we walked inside. "But that doesn't mean they all are."

We made it to the entry, where we had to choose the difficulty level for the corn maze, and Cooper turned to me. "Which one do you want to do?"

"Hmm." I studied the three different trails, which essentially boiled down to easy, medium, and hard. I pointed to the black path—the hardest one.

"I always find it interesting to see what path people choose; it says a lot about someone," Cooper said.

"You bring a lot of dates here, do you?" I led him down the left path and toward the soft, flickering glow of a lantern beckoning to us in the distance. The towering cornstalks created narrow passages and blind corners, and the outside world disappeared, leaving the two of us alone.

"I said *people* not women"—he smirked—"but that sounded an awful lot like jealousy."

Instead of looking at him, I focused on the lantern's pool of warm light that illuminated the first split in the trail. Already, the choices were starting. Though really, the choices had started a while ago. "So what did my choice say about me?"

"Obviously, that you want to spend as much time with me as possible." He squeezed my hand and shot me a flirty grin.

"It's embarrassing how easily you can read me," I said in a deadpan voice as we turned left. The ground under our feet was soft yet slightly uneven, and dry leaves occasionally crunched underfoot.

He laughed, and the rustling leaves of the stalks around us mirrored the sound. "I'd guess you don't like taking the easy path."

That felt painfully true in a lot of areas in my life, but not necessarily by my own choosing. "What would you have picked?"

"Probably the same one," he said. "I enjoy a good challenge."

"I can believe that, considering how you asked me out not long after I told you I wasn't into dating."

He smirked again. "And look at you now. On a date with me."

I rolled my eyes. "Tell me more about yourself."

"What do you want to know?"

We reached another split in the trail, and this time, Cooper picked left.

"Family? Friends? Hobbies?" I reached out and dragged a finger along the stalks of the corn looming overhead. The tiny, stiff hairs prickled against my skin, but their sweet scent filled the air.

"Seb and I grew up in Maine. Our mom left when we were little, so our dad raised us. He was busy working a lot, so Seb took care of me. But when Dad died a few years ago, we decided to start over someplace new and moved to Whisper Hollow."

"I'm sorry." I gave his hand a gentle squeeze and tried to picture a young Sebastian taking care of an even younger Cooper. Did Sebastian have his secrets even then?

"It's okay. There are fewer temptations here . . . or at least there were," he added with a small smile.

Though I wondered what sort of temptations he was talking about, now didn't seem like the right time to ask.

"Things were hard before, but they're better now." Now that we were too far from a lantern, shadows hid Cooper's expression. "Seb was always super stressed and couldn't settle down, and I had a hard time getting along with people."

My eyes widened, but I could sort of see them having to move to help Sebastian. "One of those things seems harder to believe than the other. I can see Sebastian being easily misunderstood, but you?"

He laughed softly. "Yeah, I sort of got into trouble as a teen. Wrong crowd and all that. But that was a while ago." He gave me a small smile and held a finger to his lips. "Don't tell Seb I told you this, but I'm grateful he got us out of there. Things are a lot better for both of us here. Now all that stuff is in the past."

"Just because things are in the past doesn't mean they don't hurt." I bit my lip and looked down.

Cooper swung our hands between us. "What about you? Did you come here to take over your grandmother's shop?"

"That was the plan for a while anyway." I kicked at a fallen ear of corn on the ground. "I needed a fresh start too."

"Is what happened related to why you're against dating?"

I glanced away. "That's maybe more of a second date convo, or maybe third . . . or tenth."

"Wow, you're thinking of our tenth date already? I'm flattered."

"I, uh, didn't mean you specifically."

Cooper held his free hand over his heart. "You wound me."

"Apparently, someone needs to, or you might float away with that big head of yours."

He laughed, and the towering corn around us nearly swallowed the sound.

"But coming to Whisper Hollow seemed like a good idea. I've always loved Nana's bookshop."

"Did you come here a lot? I don't remember seeing you at all before you moved in."

"We used to come every summer when Grace—that's my older sister—and I were kids, but as we got older and life got busier, Mom and Dad brought us less and less. Eventually, going to Nana's in the summer was a treat instead of an expectation. Soon enough, it became just a memory." My throat closed up as I remembered receiving the news about Nana's passing. "And then it was too late."

He squeezed my hand again. "I'm sorry about your grandmother. She was truly a wonderful woman. I always hated how much pressure she seemed to be under from work."

"Thanks." I swallowed past the tightness in my throat and sniffed once, then turned to Cooper. "You must've been close to her too. I saw the decoration she made for you and Sebastian."

"Yeah, she was good to Seb and me when we moved in. She took us under her wing." He looked at me, his dark eyes twinkling in the moonlight. "I'm sorry I didn't realize you were her granddaughter sooner."

"That's okay. It doesn't matter."

"It matters to me," he said softly as we rounded a bend. "You must miss her."

"I do, but being back here, back in her shop, is enough." I wiped my eyes and smiled up at him, then dropped my first hint. "Nana left me a letter when I got here and said she left some money for me to help get by with the shop. It's missing right now, though."

"Oh no. How much was it?"

"Honestly, I have no idea." I shrugged.

"Let me know if there's anything I can do to help you find it."

"I will." I gave him a small smile. "And while it sucks, since it would've been nice to use for the building purchase, I'll admit that searching for it has at least gotten me out and around town, which I might not have done on my own."

Cooper pulled on my hands so I came to a stop next to him. "I'm sorry for everything that's happened, but I'm glad you moved here."

"Thanks." His intense gaze held me like an embrace. The air was crisp with the feel of autumn and a sense of anticipation the longer we looked at one another.

He took a step closer, halving the distance between us, and my heartbeat thundered in my ears. It had been eight months since I'd kissed anyone. Was I ready? Was it a good idea?

"Are you glad you're here too?" His gaze dropped to my lips, then back to my eyes.

"Here in Whisper Hollow or here in this corn maze?" I said to cover the way my pulse raced. Was it a good idea? Should I let Cooper kiss me even though I wasn't sure how I felt or if I was ready for it?

His lopsided grin came out, and he gently put a hand on my cheek and rested his forehead against mine. "Here with me."

I pushed aside my hesitations and let myself melt into his touch. The wind rustled the cornstalks, then everything fell silent, as if the maze also awaited my answer.

"Yes," I whispered. I wanted to enjoy this moment.

"You're not going to pepper spray me, are you?" he asked with a small smile.

I started to shake my head, but he was already pressing his lips to mine in a soft, sweet kiss.

Someone bumped into us. "Oh, sorry," a little girl said. "I didn't see you kissing there."

I flushed and stepped back.

"Come back, Lila!" A woman with a gaggle of children came around the bend.

"Oh, Jessie, hi," I said. "Good to see you again."

Instead of exercise clothes, she wore a flowing dress embroidered with beadwork.

"You too, though you look like you're having a more relaxing and enjoyable evening than I am." She glanced down at my and Cooper's entwined hands and winked.

"The kids seem to be having a blast at least." Under her scrutiny, I tried hard to resist the urge to pull my hand free.

"Yes, well, they've been begging to come, so I offered to take them tonight." She sighed and ran a hand through her hair, making the collection of silver bangles on her arm jingle softly. "They were supposed to go last week, but then Jake had an accident and his mom had to take him to the hospital."

"Oh no." I scanned the kids as they ran around until I found the one with a cast on his arm. "I'm glad he's doing better."

"Me too."

A little girl ran up to Cooper and wrapped her arms around his leg while another little boy scampered up to Jessie. "Jessie, why didn't Nancy come too?"

"Nancy?" I asked.

"Yes, Nancy came over and watched the kids that night since I was gone." Even though she'd been working at a booth, she called in help and drove over right away, no questions asked." Jessie glanced at Cooper. "Weren't you the one who helped cover her booth?"

"Yup—"

My heart pounded, drowning out the rest of Cooper's reply. "Wait, what night was that?"

"The night of the town festival." Jessie shook her head. "Nancy is a doll."

I stiffened. That was the night Mr. James was murdered. Which meant both Nancy and Cooper had an alibi. I'd been right all along.

Now I was left, once again, suspectless.

Chapter 17

Friends in Disguise

The days after my date with Cooper passed all too quickly, and soon it was the night of the Halloween party. While I'd seen Cooper a few times in passing, I'd been so busy with party prep that we'd hardly had a chance to talk, which might've been a blessing in disguise. His kiss had helped me realize that I didn't feel anything beyond friendship for Cooper, and I wasn't looking forward to figuring out how to tell him that.

"Cupcakes?" María asked as we gave the store a final run-through.

"Nancy dropped them off an hour ago," I said over the sound of "Monster Mash" playing in the background. "They're on the table with the Frankenstein finger foods and the Edgar Allan Poe Potion Punch you made. Thanks for the tip about renaming the drink, by the way." The freshly brewed apple cider filled the shop with a sweet and spicy aroma.

"No problem. What about the smoke machine?"

"Over by checkout with the little photo booth." I gestured toward the counter of decorations.

Jiji wandered over and sniffed the stuffed black cat.

"Games?" María asked as she plugged in the string of purple and orange lights draped across the ceiling—we had also decorated the bookshelves to encourage people to check out the books.

"Jessie and Kyle are running them on the second floor."

Jiji meowed and wove between my legs, completing my outfit as Kiki, which I'd been able to throw together with a black dress and a red bow. I petted her and looked around the shop. Everything was in place, and it was time to see how many people would come.

"Then here's to hoping tonight goes well," María said.

"Agreed." Because my meeting with the bank was only two days away, and I still hadn't made much progress with finding Nana's missing money. After seeing how wrong I'd been about Nancy, I'd decided to leave finding the killer to the police. Cooper and Nancy had alibis, but it didn't explain why she'd been acting weird. Could it have something to do with what she'd promised to tell me? Maybe I could still figure it out, but constantly suspecting my friends and those around me was driving me crazy.

A woman with her two kids—dressed as a tiny ghost and a little witch—walked in, pulling me from my troubled thoughts. The kids shouted, "Trick or treat!"

"What great costumes." I pointed toward the skeleton holding the cauldron of candy. "I think those outfits deserve some candy."

They squealed and ran over, leaving me with the mother, who looked around the empty store. "We heard there was a party. Is it still happening?"

"It just started. You're the first to arrive." I gave her a wide smile. "There are games upstairs for kids, snacks here by the front, and places to take photos or check out some of the books."

The two kids scattered, one running for the staircase and the other for the table of Halloween picture books I'd set up near the food.

"And what about this flier?" The mom smiled fondly at the little witch with pigtails already devouring the kids' books. "It says here I can use it to get twenty-five percent off a purchase. Is that just for the books on display?"

My smile widened. "Not at all. The discount is for any book in the shop. I've got some fun fall reads for adults in that corner over there and a variety of children's books on the second floor."

"Thank you." The mother hurried after her kids.

Another cluster of people entered, and I turned my attention to the newcomers. María was right. Hosting was a great way to get to know more people, but it was surprising how many I'd already met on my wild hunt for Nana's money. And now many of them were showing up to support me. Or maybe they'd come for Nancy's cupcakes. Either way, I was grateful.

The shop was full, music and conversation spilling into the street each time the door opened, and the games were in full swing. Quite a few people browsed the books on display, and I'd already made a handful of sales, making me grateful I'd ordered extra books. The cozy Halloween mysteries were particularly popular.

One little girl reached for what she thought was a black cat decoration, but Jiji darted away from her hand. She squealed and chased after the cat but quickly lost her in the smoke slithering across the floor. It gave the shop a delightfully eerie atmosphere since the black light made the fog come alive with an almost ethereal glow.

"Happy Halloween," a deep voice said behind me.

I spun around to find Sebastian at the counter.

My heart jumped to my throat. "What are you doing here?"

His eyebrows shot up. "Should I not have come?"

I was grateful for the darkened room, which hid my blushing cheeks. "No, of course not. That's not what I meant." I sucked in a deep breath and let it out slowly. "I'm surprised. You said you didn't like Halloween."

Could I not have one conversation with Sebastian where I wasn't unexpectedly wearing half a sweater, accidentally spraying him with pepper spray, wrongfully accusing him of murder, or massively embarrassing myself in general?

"I know, but you're having a Halloween party, so it felt right," he said. "And I said I wasn't the biggest fan of decorating for Halloween, not that I didn't like it."

"I see." I peeked over his shoulder, trying to find Cooper's familiar head of black hair in the crowd of people moving around the darkened shop. Nerves writhed in my stomach at the thought of seeing him now that I'd decided I wasn't interested in him.

"Coop isn't here yet, if that's who you're looking for." He smiled ruefully. "He had some stuff to take care of but wanted me to tell you he'd swing by later."

"Is that the reason you came?"

"That's not what I said." He looked down and rubbed his jaw. "Your cat found me again."

I walked around the counter to find Jiji winding herself between Sebastian's legs, her tail wrapping around him and into the air. "She must like you. She doesn't normally do that."

"Fantastic." Sebastian grimaced and took a step back. Jiji followed him, the tip of her tail protruding above the smoke.

I giggled. "Looks like Cooper was right. Cats must have a way to pinpoint those who don't like them. She seems determined to win you over."

"It's easier for some than for others." He glanced at me, then looked back at Jiji. "She can try all she wants, but it won't change my allergies." He shook his head. "This is why cats are ridiculous. They only try when you don't care, but as soon as you want them, they play super hard to get."

A hint of bitterness tinged his tone, reminding me of how I'd felt after Tate's betrayal. It sounded like he was talking about more than cats.

"Well, it was nice of you to come," I told him. "If you like a good spooky read, feel free to check out some of the books on the tables."

"I'm more of a fantasy reader than horror," he admitted.

"Then you're in good company."

The lights suddenly cut out, plunging the store into darkness. The music cut off, and a smothering wave of silence fell. Someone screamed, and then a little kid cried out.

"What's going on?" Sebastian asked.

"I don't know. This wasn't part of the plan." My heart pounded as the darkness pressed in on me in a smothering wave. "Maybe the power went out. I should check—"

A loud creak sounded in front of me, and my stomach clenched. I stepped closer to Sebastian, and his strong fingers enveloped mine. My racing pulse slowed a smidge.

The black light flickered back on, the sole source of illumination in the room. Someone screamed again. "Someone's on the floor!"

"Are they hurt?" someone shouted. "Call an ambulance!"

From my position, the only thing I could see was a pair of leggings sprawled across the ground, partially hidden by the smoke. The sight reminded me too much of the morning I'd come in and found Mr. James's body on the ground. My breathing turned shallow, and I couldn't move.

"It's okay, Harp. I'm here." Sebastian's thumb brushed against the back of my hand to match his low, comforting tone.

Another loud creak filled the room, sending shivers up my spine. I whipped my attention toward the front door, but it wasn't open.

Sebastian squeezed my hand, but my pulse was racing.

The heavy thump of footsteps echoed through the room, followed by a crash of thunder.

"Wait a minute," Sebastian muttered as a howl sounded, "is this . . . ?"

The legs under the table twitched, and slowly the person rose to their feet. The smoke hid most of their legs, and they walked toward the center of the store with jerky movements.

The beginning of "Thriller" started to play, and a weird high-pitched laugh slipped from me as the room suddenly shed its tension. There wasn't anything wrong. Someone, probably María, had organized a flash mob for the party.

"I take it you weren't in on this?" Sebastian murmured in a low voice as more people started crawling and stiffly walking toward the middle of the room.

"Not at all."

He smirked. "Cooper mentioned you weren't the biggest fan of surprises."

They'd talked about me after our date? I looked up at him, then my attention fell to our hands—which were still connected.

"Oh, sorry." Sebastian pulled his hand free, and I immediately missed the warmth from his fingers.

"That's okay." I turned and watched the people dancing in the middle of the room, but I was still hyperaware of Sebastian next to me. I flexed my fingers at my side, trying not to think of how it had felt when he'd held my hand. Or, more importantly, how it had felt different from when Cooper had held my hand. The way I hadn't wanted to let go and how my pulse had raced, and not completely because of the fear of the moment.

More people wandered in from the street as if drawn by the sounds of "Thriller," and once the song ended, everyone clapped and cheered as the zombies took a bow.

"So did Cooper say anything else about the other night?" I asked as nonchalantly as I could.

"He had a lot of fun." Sebastian smiled. "Thanks for helping take care of him. I know he can be a handful sometimes. You're like Bettye."

I grinned at the compliment. Nana was good at taking care of everyone. "I'm glad you guys moved here."

"Me too." Sebastian met my gaze, and we held eye contact until my heart started pounding. "Well, I guess I'll go check out the rest of the party before I head out."

"Sounds good." I pushed away a pang of disappointment and smiled at him. "Thanks again for coming."

He walked over to the fantasy section and ducked under a hanging cobweb before he started examining the books.

The door opened—I'd taken the bell down for the party since María had insisted it took away from the Halloween atmosphere—and Sheriff Warner walked in with his family: three little boys and a teenage girl on a cell phone.

"Hi, Sheriff. I didn't expect to see you here," I said.

"My boys were begging me to take them out tonight, and since I have to work later, this was a good short way to keep my promise."

"I see." I gestured around. "Well, feel free to check everything out. There are snacks and candy for the kids, games upstairs, and, of course, plenty of books." I thought about asking him if he had any updates on the case, but then I closed my mouth. I needed to focus on my shop and the people who'd come to support me. I'd let the police do their job.

The sheriff tipped his hat to me and followed after his kids. I took a moment to look around. This was the fullest the shop had ever been, and even if I didn't get all the sales, hopefully, I could encourage some customers to come back. If the fliers did their job, I'd have people coming back over the next few days to take advantage of the discount before the promo ended.

I walked behind the counter to grab another bag of candy for the front, and the smoke machine sputtered and stopped working. I swore and knelt next to it, but flipping the switch to turn it on and off did nothing. "Not tonight," I muttered.

"Having some trouble?" Cooper asked.

"When did you get here?" I looked up at him and tucked a strand of hair behind my ear.

"Just now." He knelt and put his arm around me in a one-armed hug. "I had some errands to run and popped in." He looked around at the crowded space. "Looks like things are going well."

"Yeah," I agreed, waiting for some reaction to his contact. Increased pulse. A thumping heart. Anything. I stifled a sigh as the lack of butterflies confirmed what I'd already suspected: I didn't care romantically for Cooper. "Or at least it was until a moment ago when this stupid machine stopped working."

"Again?" Cooper laughed and let go of me to turn to the machine. "You do seem to enjoy struggling with it. Let me see if I can do anything." He fiddled with it for a minute as a furrow appeared on his brow. "Hmm. I can't get it to work. I'll call Seb."

"Oh, he's over—" I looked over at the shelves, but Sebastian wasn't where he'd been a minute ago.

Cooper already had his phone out and was calling his brother. "The smoke machine isn't working. Do you think you could come look at it?" He stayed silent for a moment, then said, "Okay, thanks."

"Is he coming?" I asked.

"He's going to grab some tools from next door and see what he can do."

A few minutes later, Sebastian came back in with a toolbox. He and Cooper each knelt beside me, putting me right between the two brothers. "This it?"

"Yup." Cooper shone a cell phone's light on the machine while Sebastian worked.

"Do you think you can fix it?" I asked.

"Probably." Sebastian didn't even look up.

"Seb is great with his hands—all that woodworking, ya know?" Cooper said.

My gaze cut to Cooper, then Sebastian as he worked on the machine. They were similar, with their dark hair, sharp jaws, and straight noses. Yet they were different too. Sebastian was serious, where Cooper was joking. Sebastian was sincere, where Cooper was flirty—aw, crap. I couldn't keep dancing around the truth. I didn't like Cooper; I liked Sebastian, and I was as idiotic as Jiji, going for someone who wasn't interested instead of focusing on someone who already liked me.

I dropped my gaze from their faces to Sebastian's hands, watching him work on the smoke machine. He opened it with a screwdriver, then pulled something else from his toolbox.

I glanced at the screwdriver he pulled out and froze. The handle was blue with gray lines up the side. It was the same design as the hammer I'd found under the bookshelf—the murder weapon that had killed Mr. James.

My mind raced through the possibilities. Sebastian couldn't be the killer. It didn't make sense. It couldn't. Yet everything seemed to match up. The way he'd been so quick to want to change the subject from talking about Mr. James's plans for our building. He had tools that matched the murder weapon—something no one besides me and the police knew about. That gave him means and opportunity. He'd also been in the flower shop recently enough to have received the flier I'd found in *Inkheart*. Half of these also applied to Cooper, but it couldn't have been him. Jessie and Nancy had seen him at the festival, unlike Sebastian, who had left the festival at least once. He'd even swung by my house that night, which probably meant no one could account for his whereabouts. Not to mention, his weird behavior with that book he was often writing in; he was clearly hiding something, and he'd tricked me into feeling bad about suspecting him.

No, wait. Had I learned nothing from all my wrong accusations? No matter how bad it looked, I needed to make sure. If I could look through the toolbox and make sure the hammer was missing—the one currently still being held at the police station as evidence—I'd have the last bit of proof I needed.

"Will you hand me a wrench, Coop?"

Sebastian's question pulled me from my thoughts. This was my chance. "I'll do it."

Cooper gave me a strange look but shrugged and sat back on his heels.

I pulled the sleeve of my sweater down and rummaged in the box, careful not to touch anything. Even through my clothes, the chill of the metal tools bled into my skin. Wrenches, screwdrivers, pliers, a tape measure, a utility knife. Pretty much everything you'd expect to be there . . . except a hammer.

My stomach fell to my toes. I hadn't been wrong after all. Sebastian was the killer.

Chapter 18

Nailing Down a Confession

A hollow, nauseated feeling settled in my stomach, and I swallowed past the dryness in my throat. While I'd sort of accused Sebastian earlier, I hadn't believed it. But now the truth was staring me in the face, refusing to be ignored.

Sebastian had killed Mr. James.

Unlike my suspicions about Mr. Humphrey, which were mostly based on hearsay, and my questions about Nancy, which had some evidence but were still too flimsy, Sebastian was holding a tool that matched the murder weapon. He'd probably planted that note on Nancy's desk to throw suspicion on someone else. That would explain why the name had been ripped off the top, to keep me from figuring out the true recipient.

Now that I knew about it, the strange smell from the paper came back to me. It had smelled like pumpkin from Nancy's shop, but the other smell had been sawdust—the same thing I'd smelled when I'd run to the back of Sebastian's shop and Jiji had knocked over his project. But more than anything, it made sense for Sebastian to be guilty because I'd finally admitted my feelings for him. Maybe Grace was right, and I was cursed.

"What are you doing, Harper? That's the wrench right there." Cooper reached around me and plucked the tool from the box, then handed it to Sebastian.

"Oh, sorry." I forced a laugh and scanned the room for Sheriff Warner. Spotting his hat a few bookshelves over, some of the tension in my chest eased. I knew what I had to do, but that didn't make it any easier.

"Hey Cooper, would you find María for me and see if she and Jessie need any help upstairs?" I couldn't have him around as I questioned Sebastian. He'd be devastated if he knew his brother was behind it all. Although, I wouldn't have had the guts to send him off, leaving me to face Sebastian alone if I wasn't surrounded by people.

"I dunno if I should." Cooper studied me with pursed lips.

My heart pounded in time with the pulse of the music in the background. "Why not?"

"Identifying tools doesn't seem to be your strong suit, and Sebastian might need help."

"I've got it covered," I said with another fake smile.

"All right then. I'm leaving my brother in your questionably capable hands." Cooper rose to his feet and threaded through the crowd.

Now that he was gone, maybe Sebastian would be willing to talk.

"I think I've almost got it." Sebastian flashed me a small smile, then returned his attention to the machine.

"Great." Nerves churned in my stomach. I couldn't confront him without a plan. I needed the sheriff close enough to hear whatever Sebastian said, but I had to do it in a way that wouldn't alert Sebastian.

A minute later, he screwed on the back of the machine. He pressed the button, and smoke billowed forth, temporarily hiding his face and making him nothing more than an outline. Sebastian started to put it back on the floor near the checkout counter, but I touched his forearm.

"I was thinking it would be better to put it over here." I gestured to a bookshelf near Sheriff Warner. "Would you move it for me? I don't want to touch it again in case I break it." I forced a smile, trying to seem normal.

"Of course." Sebastian picked the machine up and gestured for me to lead the way across the room.

As casually as I could, I grabbed the toolbox, trying to seem helpful and not like I was about to use it to accuse him of murder. Again.

My legs trembled, but in the partial light, no one seemed to notice but me. I stopped when we were on the opposite side of the bookshelf that Sheriff Warner looked at with one of his boys. There was some semblance of privacy, thanks to the shelves looming over us, and I could easily hear Sheriff Warner's voice over the strains of "Oogie Boogie's Song" when he said something to his son. Hopefully, he'd hear me as easily.

"I'd better get going. I still have some work to do tonight." Sebastian put down the smoke machine, then straightened and stretched. "Thanks for letting me come. You've done a great job with the party."

My heart jumped to my throat. I couldn't let him leave now. "Wait. I, uh, I was hoping to talk to you."

"About what?"

I licked my lips. "About Mr. James."

"Oh, about the building? I thought Cooper already talked to you about that. We're more than happy to—"

"Not about buying the building, about who killed Mr. James."

Behind me, Sheriff Warner's voice cut off mid-sentence.

"I know it was you, Sebastian."

His eyes widened. "What are you talking about?"

I steeled my heart so it wouldn't be fooled by him. Not again.

"I'm talking about this." I held up the toolbox. "The tools here are a perfect match for the hammer that killed Mr. James."

"So? I'm sure tons of people have that set."

"But is everyone else missing their hammer?"

Sebastian's gaze fell to the toolbox in my hand. "What?"

"Tell me where you put Nana's money, Sebastian," I said. "Is that how you were planning on paying for your portion of the building?"

He shook his head. "I don't know what you're talking about."

"Like you don't know about the note from Mr. James that you conveniently forgot to mention."

"What note?" Sebastian clenched his jaw. He always seemed to do that when he was with me. It was as if it were somehow my fault he'd killed Mr. James.

I should have been furious he'd killed him in my shop, but all I felt was disappointed and sort of hollow. This proved it: Guys were not to be trusted no matter how quiet, rugged, or thoughtful they seemed. I blinked back tears and tried to keep my hands from shaking.

"Please stop pretending like you don't know what I'm talking about," I said a little louder. "I found the note he wrote to you, telling you about his plans to evict us all from our shops."

He just stared at me, but the more I talked it out, the clearer everything became. "You came into my shop late that night and lured Mr. James inside when he stopped to put up the note about my rent on my door. The two of you fought and made a mess of my store"—my thoughts flashed to the disarray from that morning—"and you hit him across the back of the head with the hammer. Then you stole Nana's money and left his body there for me to find, and pinned it all on me." I was breathing heavily by the time I finished.

Sebastian met my eyes for a long tense moment. What was he going to say next? Time seemed to slow as if only the two of us were in the room, but I was still faintly aware of the chatter of voices and the fact that Sheriff Warner was close by in case something happened.

"Once the police get your fingerprints, I'm sure they'll find them all over the murder weapon," I added softly.

His jaw clenched, and his gaze darted around the shop, looking for a way out.

"You're right." He swallowed, and something in his expression snuffed out. "I did it. I killed Mr. James."

Sheriff Warner came around the corner of the bookshelf, holding out a pair of handcuffs. "Sebastian Moore, you're under arrest for the murder of Marty James."

~

The next morning, I woke with a heavy head and puffy eyes from tossing, turning, and crying most of the night. I couldn't stop thinking of Sebastian's resigned expression or the shocked look on Cooper's face as Sheriff Warner escorted his brother from the building.

The party broke up soon after that as word of what happened spread around the shop. María gave everyone a goodie bag and ushered them out the door with a reminder to come back and use the party invites to get a discount on more books.

But money suddenly didn't seem so important. Yes, we'd finally found Mr. James's killer, but why did it feel like I'd lost something? Sebastian and I were hardly friends, thanks to our rocky start, but we could be, given enough time.

No, that didn't matter. I needed to stop thinking about Sebastian. I had to talk to Nancy and see what she thought about the sale of the building now that Sebastian was out. After climbing out of bed, I fed

Jiji, who was meowing and batting at a loose string that dangled from my sleep shorts.

Despite how sluggish my body felt, I went for a quick run to wake up, then showered and biked into work. Now that the danger was past, there was no reason not to, and it served as one more way for me to put off confronting the events from the night before.

The morning mist clung to the fields like a delicate veil and added an air of mystery to the surroundings. Except the mystery was over—I'd found the killer. All I needed to do now was figure out where Nana's money had ended up.

I shivered as I biked down the sleepy streets. The leaves crunched under my tires, releasing a rich, earthy scent that mingled with the fresh, chilly air. Not quite ready to talk about things yet, I didn't call Grace on my way to work.

Even with having to get off my bike and walk it the last few feet to the top of the hill, I made it back to Whispering Pages all too soon. After locking up my bike, I walked into Sugarplum Delights. The bakery was abuzz with the gossip.

Quite a few conversations died off as I walked in, making it painfully obvious they had been talking about the arrest. I tried not to make eye contact with anyone as I made my way to the front.

Nancy gave me a sympathetic smile at the counter. "How are you holding up, hun?"

"I've had better mornings," I admitted as the conversations resumed behind me, albeit at a much lower volume than what they had been before.

"I know what you mean." Nancy shook her head. Her graying hair hung in limp curls to her shoulders as if it, too, was saddened by the events at my party. "I never would've expected it of Sebastian. That boy's never been anything but good and helpful around here."

"People can surprise you," I murmured. And it was rarely in a good way. "I don't know why he did it. I mean, I get it about the building, but why go through the trouble of framing me and leaving the body in my shop only to go speak to the sheriff later and give me an alibi?"

Nancy came around the counter and pulled me into a hug. I sniffled into her shoulder, though I wasn't even sure why I wanted to cry.

"It'll be all right, dear." Nancy patted my back. "We'll get through this."

"I know," I mumbled into her shoulder, relieved I'd never accused Nancy of murder. I could only afford to alienate so many friends.

"What you need is one of your favorite pumpkin spice lattes."

"Thank you." I fidgeted with the hem of my shirt while she bustled behind the counter. "Why were you acting so weird lately? What was it you had to tell me?"

Nancy looked down, almost guiltily. "I haven't been completely honest with you."

My stomach dropped. "About what?"

"About Bettye's money." She rifled through a drawer before pulling out a letter. "I've been meaning to give this to you."

"What is it?" I accepted the envelope and looked down at Nana's curling script across the front that spelled out my name.

"One last letter from Bettye that should explain everything." She smiled broadly. "Now, with that off my chest, we can focus on our meeting with the bank this afternoon."

"Speaking of the bank, why didn't you tell me about that note from Mr. James? You didn't have to keep it a secret." I ran a finger over the edge of the envelope, then opened it slowly. Maybe it held the rest of the answers I'd been searching for.

"What note?" Her eyebrows pulled together.

"The one about his plans to evict us—it pretty much said the same thing we heard at the bank." I pulled the letter from the envelope.

She shook her head. "I didn't see anything from Marty."

"That's weird." I mulled over the oddity of it, but then Nancy kept going.

"But anyway, with Sebastian out, I'm not sure if Cooper still plans on taking over. He was in here the other day, helping me with some boxes in my office, and he mentioned something about their finances, but—"

Her words jolted through me, and I gaped at her. "Wait a minute. Cooper was in your office the other day?"

"Yes, why?"

"Because I found that note from Mr. James in your office last week when I came by to pick up the form for the cupcakes."

"You found it in *my* office? How strange."

But my thoughts churned through everything from the last few weeks. The morning I'd run into Cooper coming out of Sugarplum Delights the day after discovering Mr. James's body in my shop. How he'd been constantly asking for updates on the case—trying to see if I was close to finding out about *him*. When he'd known exactly where the spare key in my office was the night of our date.

My stomach dropped as I put it together. Kyle had even told me Cooper had stopped by the day after we'd met. Cooper had left me a note on my desk, probably at the same time he'd slipped the key back into its place.

"We should talk to Cooper and see what he's planning," Nancy said, oblivious to my thoughts. "I know it's terrible timing, but we only have one more day to prepare for the auction."

All I could think about was the surprised look in Sebastian's eyes the night before and how his gaze had darted around the shop as if looking for someone. No, not *someone*. For his little brother. I'd thought he was trying to find some way out, but what if he'd been piecing everything together? Cooper always did say how Sebastian was an overprotective big brother.

Except, once again, I'd been wrong about things. So wrong.

"Sebastian took it too far," Nancy continued. "Surely, he had to know he'd be caught, and then his brother would be left alone. I know those brothers would do anything for each other, but he wasn't doing Cooper a favor."

"You're right." Her words were the final piece I needed. "They would do anything for each other." One of them was willing to kill to protect their business, and the other was willing to take the fall to protect his little brother. Sebastian hadn't admitted to the murder until I'd mentioned how his fingerprints were probably all over the hammer used to kill Mr. James, but if I was right, that meant Cooper's were probably on it too.

I sucked in a deep breath to steady myself. "Who covered your booth the night of the town festival when you watched Jessie's kids?"

"Cooper." Nancy pursed her lips. "Though, Sebastian did mention that he covered for his brother for a bit."

My stomach dropped. He'd covered for his brother all right . . . and I'd screwed everything up.

Nancy held a hand to my cheek. "Are you all right? You look pale."

"Oh, Nancy." I breathed slowly through my nose, trying not to pass out. "I think I've made a terrible mistake."

Chapter 19

The Hunt

"You have to listen to me," I pled with Sheriff Warner half an hour later, after rushing to the station. "Sebastian is innocent."

His nostrils flared. "What are you talking about? Sebastian already confessed to the crime."

"Because, like I said before, he's trying to protect Cooper." I stared him down, determined not to lose the argument, not when an innocent man's life was at stake. I'd already given him all the evidence I had pointing to Cooper. There was nothing else I could do to get him to believe me except pray for a miracle.

"She's right," someone said as they opened the door and walked into the sheriff's office.

"Cooper?" I jumped from my seat and took a step back. "What are you doing here?"

"Keeping my brother from throwing his life away." His eyes had none of their usual sparkle or humor. Instead, dark circles sat under them. Cooper turned to Sheriff Warner, his head high despite the slump in his shoulders. "I was the one who killed Mr. James, and my brother is trying to take the fall for me."

Sheriff Warner ran a hand over his mostly bald head and gave us an exasperated look. "What is going on here?"

"I'm telling you I'm the guilty one and my brother is innocent. I can prove it too."

"You're going to prove that you're guilty?" The sheriff's brows drew together.

Cooper smiled grimly. "If that's what it takes to keep my idiot brother out of jail."

Sheriff Warner sighed. "For now, I'll put you back in the cells."

"And my brother?" Cooper asked as Sheriff Warner handcuffed his hands behind his back.

"If you're telling the truth, he'll be out before the night's over," he said. "Unlike you."

I stepped forward before he pulled Cooper from the room, heart pounding uncomfortably in my chest. "Wait."

Both men stopped, and Cooper lifted his eyes to mine, regret darkening his gaze. A flicker of vulnerability broke through his expression before he steeled it once more.

"How did you do it?" My voice trembled, and I cleared my throat. "You had an alibi—I know you took over for Nancy at her booth."

He shrugged, but it didn't hide the tension in his shoulders. "I had someone cover at the booth for a bit."

"But why me?" Why had he tried to frame me and then date me? My hands clenched into fists at my sides.

He grimaced, more regret slipping through his mask. "I'm sorry, Harper. I honestly had no idea that it would be you taking over Bettye's shop. I thought it would be some stranger who moved in."

"So once you got to know me, you decided to try to shift the blame to Nancy?" I took a step back.

"It wasn't right. I know that, but I needed someone who had as much motive as I did."

"You shouldn't have done that." My whisper barely came out. Even now that I knew the truth, I still couldn't imagine Cooper killing someone with a hammer. It was so . . . Violent.

"I know." He shook his head, his clenched jaw making him look too much like Sebastian. "But when he delivered that note about evicting us, I knew I couldn't let him take our shop. Not after Seb and I had worked so hard to get back on our feet. Not when things were finally going well. Whisper Hollow has been good for us, and I couldn't stand the thought of things going back to how they were when I was getting into trouble all the time." His hands clenched into fists, locked in the cuffs, and his voice grew rough. "And when I overheard him mention he'd be swinging by your shop that night to deliver your notice, it seemed like a good time to talk to him away from Sebastian and our shop and everything. I didn't want Seb to have to worry anymore."

"He'll always worry about you; you're his brother." My heart ached for the bond they shared—the bond that might be irreparably broken.

"I messed up. I know." Cooper sighed and met my gaze again with a grim smile that didn't reach his eyes. His gaze looked fractured, like he'd lost a piece of himself.

That night at the corn maze, how had I not realized how deep his pain ran? Was it like that before he killed Mr. James, or was it a result of his crime?

"Will you take care of Seb for me, for real this time?" he said softly.

"I'll try," I whispered, remembering his last words before leaving Sebastian and me alone at the party.

"And Harper, I'm sorry," he said. "I know it doesn't make up for anything, but I do like you."

"You're sorry that you killed him, or you're sorry that you tried to pin it on me?"

"I'm sorry for all of it. I didn't mean to kill him. Our argument just got out of hand so fast, and then he was on the ground and I panicked and—" He broke off and closed his eyes, pulling in a shuddering breath. "Anyway, I'm sorry."

But did being sorry mean that he'd change it if he could, or was he only sorry he'd been caught?

Sheriff Warner pulled him from the room, leaving me alone with a confusing mix of emotions swirling inside me. One brother was now free, but the other would pay for his own mistake for a long, long time.

~

That afternoon, I went home without bothering to go back to the shop. I needed a distraction, and going back to the place where I'd found the body and then gotten Sebastian unjustly accused of murder was a terrible idea.

At home, I finally pulled out the letter Nancy had given me.

Dear Ink-Harp,

Before you read any further, let me apologize for not telling you about my cancer. I didn't want the family to worry about me, and I also didn't want your last memories of me to be from when I was sick and weak and looked like a dried-out noodle. I wanted you all to remember me the way I used to be.

But moving on, please go to my room and find the loose floorboard under my bed. There's a crowbar under my mattress you can use to lift it if you have trouble.

Well, that was weird. But also not *too* weird for Nana. I resisted the urge to keep reading as I made my way up to Nana's room. I ran a hand along the smooth wooden beams as I climbed the stairs. They gave the cabin a rich, earthy tone that complemented the fall decorations, like the dried cornhusks and sunflowers decorating the window at the top of the stairs. Barefoot, I walked across the plush rugs that covered the wood floor before stopping in front of Nana's bedroom. I hadn't been in there since moving in. Seeing it empty made it too real that she was gone. But it was time to accept that.

I sucked in a deep breath and pushed the door open.

Her dresser sat along one wall, a combination of old family photos and random knickknacks cluttering the top, including a bag of potpourri. A large bookshelf took up most of the far wall next to the window, and a rocker sat next to it. I smiled, remembering the many times Nana had held me in her lap and rocked back and forth while she read story after story to me.

Shaking the memory off, I turned to her bed, which took up most of the space. A large autumn-colored handmade quilt rested across the top of it, and a wreath made of dried leaves, twigs, and tiny pine cones hung above it.

The loose floorboard under her bed squeaked quietly as I pulled it free. With my cheek to the floor, I stretched one arm into the hole. My fingers brushed against something dry and papery, so I pulled it out.

A bundle of rolled cash sat in my hands.

I stared at it blankly for a moment, then reached into the hole again and felt tons of bundles. Nana had stashed who knows how much money under her bed. Was it the missing money from her shop, and she'd misplaced it after all?

I dropped the money and picked up the letter from the floor.

Congratulations! You've solved the mystery of my missing money.

Thank you for indulging your silly old grandma for one last time. You know I love a good mystery, so I wanted to give you the chance to solve one too.

Wait a minute. I blinked down at Nana's small, curling script covering the page. Was she saying what I thought she was saying, and the whole thing had been set up from the start?

I know you don't love mysteries as much as Grace and I do, but I couldn't resist the chance to set this scavenger hunt up. I'm sorry for sending you all around town like that, but you have to admit, you probably felt like a real detective, right?

Little did she know I'd be stuck in the middle of a murder case.

And I'll admit, I was a little worried that you'd get too caught up in running the business and then not find time to go out and meet anyone. Whisper Hollow is full of wonderful people (two that happen to work right next door to me), so I thought I'd take the chance to introduce you to some of my favorite places and people in town. I wanted you to make some friends. I know you struggle with being social sometimes.

I winced but kept reading. Leave it to Nana to be brutally honest.

I've been saving over the years, in case the chance ever came for me to buy Whispering Pages for real. But Marty, the old skinflint, always refused to sell. Even still, I'm happy to be able to leave this money to you to help you with the shop however you need. I'm sure you will do great things with it.

With bunches of my love and books,

Nana

P.S. Be sure to give Nancy a hug for helping me pull this off. I couldn't have done it without her.

I dropped the letter again and shook my head. I couldn't believe Nana had set that whole crazy thing up. Though, now that I thought about it, it really had been a scavenger hunt around town, leading me from one point to another.

Reaching under the bed again, I pulled out bundles of cash until the space beneath the floorboard was empty.

Then I spent the next half hour organizing the rolls of Benjamins. Careful counting proved there were forty-five stacks, and each one contained precisely fifty bills . . . meaning Nana had left me with two hundred and twenty-five thousand dollars.

Nana never had the opportunity to buy Whispering Pages, but with her help, I now had enough to pay for my portion in cash. I wouldn't even have to worry about getting a loan.

In celebration, I slept in the next morning. Well, not truly since Jiji still woke me up at the crack of dawn, but this time, she didn't wake me until the sun was up.

I went for my usual run, then biked into town for our meeting at the bank.

The gentle hum of my tires and the chirping of birds broke morning's stillness, but it sounded like the promise of a new day and a fresh start. For the first time, I didn't have to worry about a killer being on the loose. Whisper Hollow had returned to the peaceful town it was meant to be.

Despite the tranquility of the morning, butterflies fluttered in my stomach at the thought of seeing Sebastian again. I hadn't seen him since my accusation at the party, and now that Cooper was officially behind bars, I wasn't sure how he would react to seeing me.

I puffed up the hill while my thoughts chased each other in worried circles. Would he be mad at me? Upset with the hand I'd played in getting his brother arrested, even though Cooper had come forward on his own to confess in the end?

At the top of the hill, the roads were mostly deserted except for a few other cyclists and some joggers coming out of their houses. I pressed on the brake and screeched to a stop, looking back down the path while huffing for breath. I'd been so consumed with thoughts of

Sebastian that I hadn't even realized I'd finally made it to the top of the hill without stopping.

"I did it," I said softly before shouting it again, "I did it! Woohoo!" My cry caused a few birds to take off in startled flight from a nearby tree, rustling the branches so some red and orange leaves drifted over me.

I couldn't believe I'd finally done it. Somehow, that happening on top of everything else, felt like yet another sign I was meant to stay in Whisper Hollow. I had the money for the bookshop, I'd solved the murder and made it up the hill, and even more impressive, I'd made a few friends. It was time to stay and give my life in the small town a real shot.

Grinning, I continued biking to the bank, taking a road other than Main Street. Outside, I locked up my bike, then turned to the door and ran into Sebastian as he got out of his car.

"Oh, hi." There were those butterflies again. Darn them.

"Hey." He looked at me, then looked down at the sidewalk, his shoulders slumped.

Nerves killed off the butterflies. Would Sebastian forgive me for what I'd done? Was there any way for us to be friends now?

I studied him from the corner of my eye, my heart sinking as I took in his wrinkled shirt and the bags under his eyes. He'd had an even worse night than I had.

A bubble of awkward tension grew between us for a moment until I couldn't take it anymore.

"I'm sorry." The words spilled from me at the same time Sebastian said, "I'm sorry about Coop."

"Wait, what?" I cocked my head to the side and looked at him.

He drove a hand through his hair, making the disheveled strands stand out even more. "No, you first."

"I'm sorry for what happened," I said.

"That's my line." He sighed. "I shouldn't have taken the blame for him at the party, but when I realized what you were saying, and that Coop was behind it all, I panicked, and my mouth spoke without my brain catching up."

"You're used to taking care of him," I said softly.

"Maybe too much." Sebastian frowned and scuffed his shoe along the ground. "He's always struggled with impulse control, and I've always helped him fix his problems, but I never believed he'd do something like that."

Impulse control. That explained his forward behavior and how he never seemed to sit still. All the times he'd flirted with me, I'd thought he was confident, but maybe he also blurted things out without considering the consequences.

"He'd been doing so well since coming here. Whisper Hollow has been the perfect place for us." He ran a hand through his hair again. "I should have seen the signs. I should have done better, cared for him better. How can I–" He cut himself off and sucked in a sharp breath, still not looking at me. "Anyway, I'm sorry for everything Coop and I have put you through. Bettye would be ashamed of us."

"That's not true." I put a hand on his arm. "Nana was great at pinpointing people's weaknesses with an eagle eye, but her real strength was that she could also find someone's strength. And she loved you two—I can tell in the way she talked about you in her emails."

Sebastian blinked and cleared his throat. "Well, thank you. That means a lot."

Since the brothers had lost their parents, it probably did mean a lot. Nana might've been as much a grandmother to them as she was to me.

It was that thought that gave me the courage to slide my hand down his arm and grab his hand, a gesture of comfort. "I know what it's like to have someone you love betray you, so if you need anything, I'm here for you."

"Thanks." He gently squeezed my hand, the calluses of his fingers brushing against my fingers.

I bit my lip and looked down at our hands.

Behind us, someone cleared their throat. "I'm not interrupting anything, am I?"

Sebastian and I spun around to find Nancy standing behind us with her hands on her hips. She winked in a way-too-obvious manner.

"Not at all." Sebastian pulled his hand free and opened the door for us, but I didn't miss the way he flexed it at his side or how it made my heart flutter. "After you, ladies."

Nancy took my arm and led us into the bank as she whispered none-too-quietly, "You sly thing."

"Nancy, it isn't like that." Or was it? "I was telling him I'm here for him if he needs anything since I'm sure it's hard for him to be without Coop right now."

"Anything, indeed." Nancy winked. "I'm glad you two are making the most of this terrible situation."

I shook my head and gave up on trying to set her straight. Nancy was going to believe whatever she wanted to believe, regardless of what I said.

"Seby, is that you?" An elderly lady with a head of fluffy white hair came toward us with a walker.

I gave him a wide-eyed look and mouthed, "Seby?"

Sebastian's eyes widened. "Mrs. Schoenfield, what are you doing here?"

"I had to deposit a check, and I couldn't remember that thing you showed me with my cell phone, so I came in person to ask for help." She reached up and patted Sebastian's cheek with a wrinkled hand, though he had to bend down slightly so she could reach. "You've already been so much help, and I didn't want to bother you again with everything going on with Cooper."

"Wait"—I looked between them in confusion—"how do you two know each other."

"This and that," Sebastian mumbled.

Mrs. Schoenfield laughed. "Don't be modest, boy." She turned to me. "Sebastian comes by the nursing home about once a week to help the residents with different things."

"What?" My stomach dropped for an entirely different reason. How was I supposed to pretend like that didn't make Sebastian the most attractive man I'd ever met?

"Ooh, he's a keeper," Nancy muttered to me. "Better snag him quick before someone else does."

"Do you have family at the nursing home?" I asked him.

Sebastian's face was red, and he wouldn't meet anyone's eyes. "No, it's something Bettye recommended I do." He ran a hand down his face and peeked at me. "She could tell I was stressed about a lot of things when we moved here, and she said one of the best ways to forget your troubles is to help someone else. So she took me to the nursing home my first month here . . . and it sort of stuck."

"And boy has he been helpful. Not only does he help us all with different projects around the center, but he also brings fresh flowers every time he visits." Mrs. Schoenfield sighed and fanned her face. "Almost makes me feel three decades younger, having a handsome man like Seby bringing me flowers every week. He even writes little notes to go with them."

That was why his name was on the Blossom Boutique registry? Because he was taking flowers to the nursing home? And were those notes what he was writing in that notebook he refused to let me see? My heart melted a little more.

"They're for everyone," Sebastian muttered.

"Don't ruin this for an old lady." She smiled and patted his arm. "Anyway, I won't keep you. I'm sure you've got plenty to do today, but I'm looking forward to seeing you on Sunday."

Sebastian ducked his head, and Mrs. Schoenfield walked through the door with a quiet cackle.

Mr. Thomas walked out of his office and saw the three of us standing by the door. "Are you ready for the auction? It'll start in a few minutes."

"Be right there," Sebastian told him.

"Well, shall we?" Nancy asked as Mr. Thomas walked off.

I swallowed the nerves that sprouted as I thought about how much money I was about to spend and grabbed the handle of the bag over my shoulder—the bag carrying Nana's no-longer-missing money.

"Let's do it." Sebastian strolled forward without looking back, but it didn't hide the red tips of his ears.

Nancy followed after him, and I studied them as I followed them in to purchase Whispering Pages and make it officially mine. Not only had I saved Nana's shop—well, technically she'd saved it—but I'd finally made her dream of owning it come true. It was the least I could do for her bringing me to Whisper Hollow.

Nana had been right. My life here was full of as much adventure as any of the books at Whispering Pages, and I couldn't wait to see what the next chapter held.

~ The End ~

The mystery may be solved, but one question remains: What did you think of the story? Your review can help other readers crack the case of deciding their next cozy mystery read. Please write a review (even just one line) or leave a rating on Amazon, Goodreads, or Bookbub.

Join my mailing list for a <u>bonus scene</u> that takes place before book one

or join my list for <u>Harper and Jiji character art.</u>

To find out what happens next in Harper's story, check out *<u>Murder With a Hint of Peppermint</u>*.

About the author

Laura Drake is the youngest of five and grew up in Arkansas until she moved to Provo, Utah to attend Brigham Young University. She graduated with a degree in elementary education and worked as a fourth-grade teacher before moving to Tokyo for a few years. She writes in a variety of genres because there are too many good ones out there to limit herself and she enjoys trying new things. When she isn't writing, she enjoys reading, playing ultimate frisbee and board games, and spending time with her family and friends. She is passionate about time management and loves helping people make budgets.

Laura is a member of The Church Of Jesus Christ of Latter-day Saints.

Use this QR code or the hyperlink to get to Laura M. Drake's linktree, which has links to all of her social media and books.

Check out
Laura M. Drake

Also by

The Chronicles of Andar trilogy— a YA trilogy where Harry Potter
meets Avatar: the Last Airbender
Japanese Haunting series— a clean spooky read that's perfect for Halloween
Till Life Do Us Part— a paranormal romantic suspense
One Dark Night — a collection of short mysteries that's perfect for a
quick, eerie read
Once Upon a Raven (COMING NOVEMBER 2024) — a collection
of short fairytale retellings with a twist

Check out
Laura M. Drake

Printed in Great Britain
by Amazon

50053818R00115